TALES OF HAPPINESS AND HEARTBREAK
ON THE PRAIRIE

MY DAKOTA

Dennis (A.K.A. Birthay Boy),

Thanks for your interest in my book.

Alan

Alan Quale

My Dakota

ISBN: 978-1-61170-026-8

Cover photo of the Little Missouri River in North Dakota by Gerald Blank (www.gblankimagery.com)

Printed in the United States of America on acid free paper.

To purchase additional copies of this book go to:
www.rp–author.com/quale

Robertson Publishing
59 N. Santa Cruz Avenue, Suite B.
Los Gatos, California 95030 USA
www.RobertsonPublishing.com

This book is dedicated to the memory of my family and friends in North Dakota.

We will be known forever by the tracks we leave.
— Dakota Sioux proverb

Table of Contents

Introduction

Like many families in the postwar era of the late 1940s and early 1950s, the Anderson family was on the move, searching for their niche in America.

While many families soon settled down in one spot, the Andersons kept moving. It seemed as though they just couldn't find a suitable place to live.

In many ways, the Andersons were a family without a home.

Then they came to Alexander. The town looked much like the others on the prairie, a small settlement with a main street lined with businesses, and dusty side streets with rows of homes.

But Alexander was unlike other prairie towns because of the land around it. There were tall hills and buttes crowned with sandstone. The landscape gave a different feel to the place, and that had a certain appeal for the Andersons.

None of them said it out loud, but this was *the place*. It was time for the prairie nomads to settle down.

Chapter 1

Thorny Welcome

Eric's first glimpse of Alexander, North Dakota, was from the rear seat of a 1948 Ford Coupe. His mother, Inga, was driving as they crossed the top of a large hill on Highway 85. The summit was crowned by scattered sandstone boulders and thinning prairie grass, dominating the landscape for miles around, with rolling prairie stretching in all directions below it.

"There it is," his mother said, one hand on the steering wheel and the other pointing at the windshield.

"Where?" Eric asked. At eight years old, Eric had to raise himself from his seat to get a better view.

"It's down there," his mother said. "Can't you see the grain elevators?"

"No. Where are they?"

Inga didn't answer; she put both hands on the wheel, following the highway down the hill. The highway made a long downhill curve before leveling off again. Then it crossed over a final hill, and the town suddenly appeared below.

The highway sliced through the middle of Alexander, and they could see the elevator buildings up ahead on the far side of town, where the land rose up again, forming a tall butte crowned with more sandstone boulders. On the side of the butte was a large letter "A" made of rocks that were painted white.

As they drove into town, Eric and his mother were silent, wondering what it would be like living there. It was a familiar feeling for them; they were accustomed to moving from one small town to the next. Eric's father, Justin Anderson, managed grain elevators throughout North Dakota and Montana, buying grain from farmers and ranchers.

Every year or two, the company that owned the elevators would transfer Justin to a new elevator, which was usually plagued by fiscal mismanagement or other pitfalls of the grain business. Justin became the company's troubleshooter, and the Andersons became prairie nomads, moving frequently.

The towns they lived in were always small. Justin called them "spots on the road," and they were scattered throughout the prairie in western North Dakota and eastern Montana.

So far, they'd lived in Opheim, Appam, Brockway, Rawson, Lone Tree and Trenton.

Their stay in Lone Tree was notably brief. They were awakened by shouts outside their house in the middle of the night. The elevator had somehow caught fire. Flames were already spreading up the exterior walls as they joined a crowd of onlookers. Within minutes the flames reached the top of the 100-foot structure, which exploded in a giant ball of burning timber and grain.

The tall inferno slowly began to tilt and then it came crashing to the ground, raising thick clouds of smoke and cinders. The adjacent tracks of the Great Northern Railroad were buried in the ruble, disrupting train service on the Northern Plains for two days.

Justin helped direct the cleanup and wrote a report for the fire inspector. Two weeks after the fire, the company asked Justin to move to Trenton, a small town near the Missouri River close to the North Dakota-Montana border. Business had fallen sharply in Trenton, and the company wanted Justin to try to turn things around. The Andersons were on the move again.

Although their stay in Lone Tree was cut short, the Andersons weren't complaining. After all, Lone Tree was a tiny hamlet with only a cluster of homes, including the elevator manager's house, a ramshackle residence that looked like an oversize bungalow. The nearest grocery store was in the next town, 12 miles away, and Eric's older sisters, Clarice, age 11, and Caroline, age 9, would have to ride a bus 18 miles to the only school in the area.

The elevator inferno may have been a disaster for the Lone Tree, but it felt like a blessing to the Andersons. Strangely enough, the burning elevator also showed the Andersons there was at least one advantage to being prairie nomads. If you ended up in a really bad place, a place like Lone Tree, you knew it wouldn't be for long.

Lone Tree became one more dot on the Andersons' map. It was followed by the family moving to Trenton for one year and then Brockway, Montana, for the following year.

And now, Eric and his mother were entering their newest town, passing a green sign on the side of the highway that said:

> Alexander
> Population 415

"That's where you'll be going to school," Inga said, pointing to a red brick building on the side of the street. The street descended past the school and a line of homes before leveling off as it entered the business area, where several stores and two gas stations lined the roadway. In the center of town was a park the size of one city block. The park was bordered by businesses on three sides. The trees in the park were full-grown, and they hung over the street, facing the businesses.

The town was nestled at the bottom of a bowl-shaped valley, with buttes and hills rising up on all sides.

"Where's our house?" Eric asked

"I don't know."

"How'll we find it?"

"We'll stop and ask."

"Who'll you ask?"

"Don't worry, I know who to ask." There was a sudden sharp edge to his mother's voice. She brushed the hair from the side of her head and shook her shoulders slightly.

It had been a long, hot drive for her from their previous home in Brockway. For Eric, the drive was endless boredom, staring out the car window at the prairie, counting the deer and antelope alongside the road. The big sky stretched forever above the treeless plains. Eric was the only passenger because his sisters had left Brockway two days earlier with their father. The plan was for Justin, Clarice and Caroline to set things up in their new home. Eric and his mother stayed on in Brockway so that Inga could clean the house before they left. Eric would stay behind to help his mother and give her some company during the long drive to Alexander.

After the hot and boring trip, they were eager to get out the car. Inga pulled the car to the side of the street next to the park. In the corner of the park stood a building with open sides and a roof supported by columns of rock rising in each corner. Inside the structure, spring water flowed out of a large metal pipe that rose up from the ground and bent 45 degrees. A steady stream of cold, clear water flowed out of the pipe, falling down into a narrow ditch that channeled the water out of the structure.

They got out of the car and were walking toward the spring when a tall man approached. He wore a farmer's cap, with John Deere spelled across the front. His dusty clothing seemed to indicate that he was somehow connected to the elevator business.

He stopped and ginned, removing his cap.

"You must be Inga," he said. "Welcome to Alexander."

Inga nodded yes to him. "And you are?"

"I'm Charlie...Charlie Stenseth. I'll be helping Justin in the grain elevator. I'm here to show you to the house."

"I hope you haven't been waiting long," Inga said.

"No ma'am." Charlie rubbed the toe of his boot in the dirt. "I was just over there." He motioned with his shoulder at the bar across the street with a red neon Budweiser sign in the window.

Inga took a long drink from the flowing spring water and then Eric had his turn. The water was ice cold and tasted good.

They all got into the car and Charlie directed them to the house, which sat only a half-block behind the business district, facing a tall hill. The house wasn't much, a plain looking building sheeted in tin, with a roof that was almost flat, sloping slightly from the front to the rear. At the front of the house was a large window, facing an alleyway that led to Main Street. Bordering the house was a large expanse of grass, probably a half-acre or more.

Justin, Clarice and Caroline were moving furniture in the living room when Eric and his mother walked into the house.

"Well, there they are," his father said. The sisters looked up briefly then continued moving a table.

Inga walked toward Justin, but they didn't embrace. Instead, they simply smiled at one another and began speaking in Norwegian. Inga and Justin's parents had all emigrated from Norway and became homesteaders on the prairie in the early 1900s. Norwegian was the first language that Inga and Justin leaned, and now, years later, they still slipped back to speaking Norwegian when they had something special to say.

Later, after most of the furniture was in place, Inga heated tomato soup and made cheese sandwiches for supper. Everyone seemed tired, but there was also a certain excitement in the air as they talked.

"The park is nice," Inga said. "And the school looks

good, at least from the outside."

"Actually, the elevator seems to be in pretty good shape," Justin said, sounding surprised. "Charlie said about 40 farmers and ranchers are doing regular business with the elevator."

"I wonder if the school is big enough to field a basketball team *and* a football team," Clarice said.

"Boys, boys, boys," Caroline teased. "That's all you think about now that you sold your horse."

Clarice scowled across the table at her younger sister and wrinkled her nose at her.

Eric was restless and didn't want to listen to any more of the family talk. He gulped down his bowl of soup and finished shoveling the sandwich into his mouth. Then he got up and left the table, with no one objecting. The Anderson family had very informal dining manners.

Eric walked out of the house and looked to the west across the large grassy area toward the big hill. The air seemed a little fresher now, much cooler than the inside of the house. There was little wind, just a slight breeze.

He set out to climb the hill. Halfway up, he realized the slope was much steeper than it had looked from below. The food he had just devoured was churning in his stomach.

As he climbed he saw patches of prairie cactus, some sprouting bright red flowers, which he gingerly stepped around. The top of the hill was surprisingly flat and nearly devoid of any vegetation, with only thinning grass. Eric stood looking down at the town below. A single car entered the town on the south side, and he watched it move slowly up Main Street and climb the hill past the school. He followed the car's ascent up the long rise to the larger butte and watched as it disappeared over the summit.

Eric looked down on the town once again. There was no traffic on the highway now and the air was still and almost silent. He heard people's voices from somewhere below, although he couldn't tell what they were saying.

The town had a certain attraction to Eric, with the park sitting squarely in the middle, the adjacent business district and the quiet residential streets fanning out toward the surrounding hills and buttes. Eric wondered if they might stay here longer than the usual. On the other hand, this could be just another brief stop on the prairie.

Satisfied with his view of the town, Eric decided to return home. It felt good to be walking after the long drive with his mother. The walk down the hillside was easy, and he began jogging slightly; then, he decided to break into a run. But as he picked up momentum he lost his footing and fell forward. He seemed to fly for an instant as the ground came rushing up at him.

Whap! He landed hard on his side and rolled forward. He was rolling out of control down the hillside, his body slapping the ground with crunching sounds. He tried to grab hold of anything to stop his fall but the momentum kept pulling him down.

Suddenly there was a prickly, stinging sensation on his backside, and moments later he finally rolled to a stop. He lay dazed on the ground and then he slowly stood.

He felt dizzy and he shook his head, trying to regain his sense of balance.

He brushed the dust from his clothes and pulled a clump of thistle weed dangling from a shirt pocket. He flung the thistle to his side in anger. Then he felt the sharp, prickly pain. It was coming from his buttocks.

He stretched his arm behind his back and slowly slid his hand downward until he felt the prick of the needles.

Oh my God, he thought, *cactus!*

Eric's buttocks began to throb; the needles seemed to press inward on his bottom. His pants and shirt were matted with the cactus, which had been ripped from the ground as he rolled. Eric turned toward his house, which suddenly looked like it was a very long distance.

As he moved forward, every step brought a new burst of pain as his clothing shifted and tugged at the needles lodged in his buttocks. He walked awkwardly, slowly moving ahead, teeth clenched and his face tightened. He was crossing the street that bordered the large grassy area when he heard the shout.

"Hi. What's your name?"

He turned to see a freckled girl approaching from behind. She rode a blue bicycle with colored strands of leather dangling from the ends of the handle bars.

"I'm Eric," he said, trying to control his face muscles as another sharp wave of pain rushed over his backside.

"Why are you walking so strange" she asked. "Are you hurt?"

"I'm just a little sore," he said. "I, uh, I fell coming

down the hill."

As she rode past him on her bike, he turned, following her, and took a few steps forward, trying to look normal. The stinging pain was growing so intense that he almost screamed.

The girl suddenly stopped her bike up ahead and turned to face him. "I'm Anita," she said, looking back at him.

"Hello," he said. As he stepped forward his movement brought another wave of incredible pain. He felt his face growing tighter.

"Are you from the new elevator family?" she asked.

"Yep," he said. His voice sounded high-pitched and tense. He wished this girl would go away. He wished he was home.

"Are you going to go to school here?" she asked, still facing him.

"Yep, I am." His voice sounded like a muffled squeal. The pain was growing worse, and he worried the seat of his pants might be covered with blood. He shifted slightly so that she could not see his back.

"So am I," she said. Her smile looked warm and genuine, but it didn't hold Eric's attention. His buttocks were throbbing with intense pain and he couldn't stand it any longer.

"Aaaaeeeeaah!" Eric's scream seemed to bounce off the hillside, and his face flashed hot. Dogs began to bark somewhere nearby.

Anita's mouth dropped open as she stood staring at

him. She seemed to be searching for an explanation.

"I...uh...I like doing that now and then," Eric said. "It feels good to let out a howl now and then."

Anita suddenly looked frightened as she mounted her bike and quickly peddled away.

"Well, see you around," he called after her. His voice was tight and high-pitched as he tried to mimic a casual goodbye.

Eric's mother was an expert at removing needles from man and beast. There was the time the family dog, an overgrown terrier named Tiny, got too close to a porcupine. Tiny foolishly tried to bite the porcupine, but ran away yelping with a nose full of quills. Inga held the dog firmly on her lap, snipping the end of each quill with scissors and then pulling each quill out with a pair of pliers. Tiny yelped again and again as his nose turned bloody, but he did not move from her lap until she was done.

Now it was Eric's turn. He lay face down on his bed, with the cactus still matted on the seat of his jeans. Eric moaned as his mother prepared herself. In one hand she held the familiar scissors and pliers and in the other a pan of water with a wash cloth draped on the side.

Eric heard the strangely familiar sounds of his mother methodically snipping needles. She severed each needle between the cactus plant and Eric's jeans and then gingerly lifted the matted cactus away from his clothing. Next she slowly pulled Eric's jeans and underwear away from his buttocks. The needles slid through the cloth and were still embedded in Eric's buttocks when she pulled the clothing down his legs. His mother paused and took a deep breath. She was ready to begin pulling the needles out.

"Aaaaeeeeaaah!" He was shocked by the sudden pain as his mother pulled the first needle out. The muscles on his backside winced and tightened. "Oh, that hurt!"

"You have got to be still," she said calmly. "I can't get them out if you move around."

Eric heard giggling sounds and looked up to see his sisters standing in the doorway to the room.

"Aaaaeeeeaaah!" He screamed again as his mother plucked another needle. He heard more giggles from the doorway and turned to face them.

"Get out of here!" he shouted. "This isn't funny!"

They still stood in the doorway, their giggles growing louder.

"Ma, get them out of here!" Eric said.

He felt his mother's weight shift on the bed as she turned, facing the door.

"Go away," she said, "now!"

He heard his sisters leaving and he breathed a little easier, but just for an instant.

"Aaaaeeeeaaah!" His mother surprised him with another yank of the pliers.

Eric's face flushed hot, and beads of sweat were forming all over his body. His mind was racing with the pain. *This must be what hell is like,* he thought.

He tried to detach himself from the scene, imagining himself somewhere up above staring down. He saw himself on the bed, his buttocks smeared with blood and his mother bent over him with a pair of pliers in her hand.

"Aaaaeeeeaaah!" Another needle was pulled and he began to twist in pain on the bed.

He felt humiliated and tortured by this ordeal. His body tensed, waiting for the next pull of the pliers.

"Aaaaeeeeaaah!" Another sharp jab of pain rippled across his buttocks. His screams were growing so loud they were likely heard by their neighbors. His mother pinched the pliers on another needle and pulled up.

"Aaaaeeeeaaah!" He let out his loudest scream yet. It was high pitched, like a woman's scream, and it seemed to bounce off the walls and reverberate into the hallway. He didn't care what it sounded like. The pain was unbelievable and it felt good to scream, the louder the better.

"It's hurting, Ma," he said. "It hurts bad!"

"I know, but you have got to be still," she said. "We're getting there."

She seemed to pause, giving him time to catch his breath as he lay moaning on the bed, breathing heavily. His buttocks were on fire and the perspiration was dripping from his body onto his drenched bed. Only his eyes remained dry. The pain was too intense for tears.

"Aaaaeeeeaaah!" His face was locked in a strange grimace and his breathing started to sound like he was panting. He wished this painful torment would soon end. He didn't know how many more cactus needles were left. *He didn't want to know.*

His body began shaking as another rush of hot pain

swept over him.

"Lay still," his mother said. "I'm almost done."

He clutched his pillow with one arm and slid his other arm over the side of the bed, grabbing the frame below.

"Aaaaeeeeaaah!" Another needle was pulled. Eric buried his face in the pillow. His buttocks felt like they were really on fire; it felt like someone tossed match and they burst into flames. His muscles were convulsing all over his body. He felt like he was going crazy with the pain.

"Okay, we're done," his mother said. Eric lay perfectly still, almost disbelieving what he'd just heard.

She gently pulled off his jeans and began washing his buttocks with the wash rag. The cool water seemed to lessen the throbbing pain, ever so little.

Eric lay exhausted on the bed, his face still buried in the pillow. Then he felt something damp nuzzle his hand on the side of the bed. There was a long wet lick up his arm. It was Tiny. He was there to provide comfort as only a dog could do. Tiny knew exactly what Eric was going through.

"Good doggie," Eric said, his voice choking on the words. He turned his head to face Tiny. The dog stood on his rear feet, placing his front paws on the bed. Then Tiny stretched his head forward and began licking the tears as they flowed down Eric's cheeks.

Later that night, long after the cactus needles had been pulled; Eric lay motionless on his side in his bed. His body felt numb, except for occasional dull throbs of pain, which seemed to grow stronger and then suddenly weaken.

Eric reflected on his first day in Alexander. He saw himself and his mother driving across the summit above the town and pulling to the side of the road at the park to be greeted by Charlie. He remembered the family chatter at super, gulping down his food and his exciting climb to the top of the big hill.

And then, the sudden plunge and the furious roll across a cactus patch filled with bright red flowers and lethal needles. Like so many things on the prairie, something beautiful could bring incredible pain. And a moment of happiness could be ruined in seconds.

Now Eric was exhausted, but he couldn't sleep because of the stabs of pain that continued to flare across his buttocks. His body remained tense, it felt like he was wound up in a tight ball and couldn't stretch out.

Still, he hoped he might soon fall asleep.

He wished he could.

Eric yawned, almost purposely, and carefully stretched his legs. Sharp jabs of pain flashed again across his buttocks. "Uuuuuhhhhh," he moaned.

He shifted slightly on his side, trying to find a more comforting position. As he lay there in the small bedroom, he suddenly felt lonely and wished there were someone to talk to. Everyone else in his family was probably asleep. Eric's only companion was Tiny, who was curled up at his feet at the foot of the bed. Even Tiny was asleep now, his legs moving with sudden jerks. The dog's ears began to twitch, a sure sign he was dreaming, probably chasing a rabbit or a prairie rat or maybe a porcupine.

A sudden flash of light illuminated the room through the window. Eric looked out at the heat lightning that was forming above the hills to the west. Purple streaks spread across the sky, illuminating the prairie below.

The lightning looked almost graceful as it laced horizontally in zigzag patterns. Eric heard thunder far off in the distance. Watching the gathering storm was exactly what he needed to take his mind away from his scarred body.

Eric's eyes were growing heavy now, but he blinked to watch another flash of lightening flash across the horizon. And then he was asleep.

Each day that followed his plunge through the cactus patch brought relief and healing to Eric's buttocks. He still stood at breakfast, dinner and super, feeling awkward as he looked down on everyone else at the table.

But he could walk okay, there was less pain and his mother said there didn't appear to be any infection.

Finally, Eric got up the nerve one morning to go out of his house. He was crossing Main Street, walking toward the park, where he saw two groups of boys, one on each side of the grassy area in the middle. Each group had several red metal wagons, which lay sideways on the grass, facing the other group.

The boys were lying prone behind the wagons. It looked like two battle lines were forming.

"Ping!" Eric heard the unmistakable sound of a BB pellet striking something. Then he saw the BB guns pointed over the tops of the wagons.

"Ping, ping, ping." The BBs were raining down on the wagons as the firefight began.

"Ouch, you bastard," cried one of the boys nearest to where Eric was standing. He stood and started to run across the open area toward the other line of wagons. The other group opened fire, sending the boy retreating back to his line of wagons as the pellets rained down. "Ping, ping, ping."

"Ow, God damn it," he cried as he dove behind a wagon. "I'm going to kick your ass," he shouted over the top of his wagon.

Eric had never heard profanity like that from a boy. In fact, he rarely heard such talk from grownups. He watched, almost transfixed, as the boy continued to holler curses and threats across the park.

"I'm going to knock your head down to your ass," the boy shouted to the opposing group of boys.

Across the park there was movement behind the other line of wagons. Suddenly the boys stood and began running from the park, their wagons dragging and banging clumsily behind them.

The boys nearest to Eric opened fire; several popping sounds from pellet guns rang out as the winners of the battle took aim at the fleeing boys.

"Ha, ha, ha, chickenshits," shouted the boy. He appeared to be the leader of his group. He stood laughing and flapped his arms like they were wings. "Ark, ark, ark, chickenshits."

Then the boy saw Eric standing nearby and began walking toward him. Eric didn't know whether he should run or stand fast.

"Who the hell are you?" the boy demanded.

"I'm Eric. We just moved here. My dad manages the elevator."

"Well, don't ever do this to me," he said. He pulled back the blond hair that hung over his forehead. A large red welt was forming in the middle of his forehead.

"I don't even have a BB gun," Eric said.

"Oh, poor boy," the boy said in a mimicking voice of a bully. "He doesn't even have a gun. Poor boy, poor boy." The other two boys started to laugh.

Eric turned and walked away, hoping the bully wouldn't follow. He breathed easier as he crossed Main Street and glanced back to see the bully and his friends still milling about in the park.

When Eric reached the sidewalk on the other side of the street he turned and began walking up the hill toward the school.

He was passing a tall house with a hedge in front when he heard a rustling noise in the hedge.

"Psst, are they still in the park?" The voice came from the hedge.

"What?" Eric asked.

"Are Keith Johnson and those guys still in the park?"

"Who's Keith Johnson?" Eric asked.

The bushes parted and a tall boy with red hair stepped

through.

"I'm Ray Sorenson," he said, grinning. Then his face turned serious. "Who are you?"

"I'm Eric Anderson. My dad manages the elevator. We just moved here."

"I was in the gang facing Keith Johnson and his boys," Ray said. "I think I'm the one who shot Keith."

"He showed me the mark on his head," Eric said. "He's real mad."

Ray's eyes grew wide. "What did he say?"

Eric hesitated. "Uhhhh, I don't know."

"Come on," Ray said. "He must have said something. I saw him talking to you."

Eric coughed before speaking. "He said he was going to knock your head down to your ass." Eric blurted out the words, somewhat amazed that he could also talk like that. Ray's eyes were growing even wider.

"Oh, my God," Ray said. "I better go home." He motioned toward Eric, "Come on, I'll show you my place."

Eric hesitated for a second then followed Ray up the street. Eric wasn't so sure he should be associating with this marked boy. But then Eric was new in town and had no friends here. Even a marked boy, a boy who seemed to want Eric's company, was better than no friend at all.

Ray's house looked imposing, rising haughtily above the smaller homes on the hillside. The house had two floors, a weathered wood exterior and a screened porch in front.

Ray's mother, a friendly looking woman with blond hair and Nordic features, greeted them at the door.

"You're just in time for lunch," she said to Ray. Then she turned to Eric. "And who are you?"

"I'm Eric. We just moved here. My dad manages the elevator."

"Can he stay for lunch?" Ray asked.

His mother turned to Eric and smiled. "Call your mother and see if it's okay," she said.

And so began Eric's friendship with Ray. In the weeks that followed, they became buddies. Ray showed Eric all the fun things to do around Alexander, and he introduced Eric to his friends, which didn't include Keith. They also explored all of the buttes that surrounded the town one by one.

Ragged Butte to the north of town was their favorite. Huge sandstone boulders dotted the top of the butte, and several caves opened from the side. "Here's Indian Cave," Ray said, pointing beneath a large rock ledge as they explored the butte. Eric might have walked right past it. The opening was so low that they had to drop to their knees and crawl in on the sandy floor. Soon they came to a bowl-shape room big enough for them to stand in. Slowly their eyes adjusted to the dim light and Eric could see two round openings in the wall about two feet above the floor.

"This is the burial chamber," Ray said, moving his arms in a wide arc. "Years ago, settlers found three dead Indians in here. They think the holes in the wall are where they stored their dead."

Ray approached one of the holes and stuck his arm inside.

"But I know something even the settlers didn't know," he said, a sly smile forming on his face. "The two holes are connected. You can climb through from this hole and come out over there." He motioned to the other hole, which was about 10 feet away in the wall.

Eric stepped forward and leaned into the hole, which curved to the left. It was dark, with a musty unknown odor.

"Get in there," said Ray, playfully pushing Eric's forward.

Eric reared back, hitting his head on the top on the opening. He pulled out of the opening and stood back, rubbing the back of his head.

"I'm not going in there," Eric said. "I don't like tight spots." He looked at Ray, waiting for him to tease him. But Ray only grinned and stepped to the hole.

"See you on the other side," he said, leaning into the opening. The small hole seemed to slowly devour Ray. His upper torso slid in first, leaving his legs bent and thrashing outside the hole. Then the legs slowly moved forward into the hole until all that was visible were the bottoms of his shoes.

Then the shoes disappeared and Eric stood alone in the cave. After a few minutes he walked to the other hole and put his head inside, listening for any sounds.

There was only silence. Eric stepped back and turned, glancing around the chamber, examining the cave more closely. He saw winding tracks on the sandy floor of the cave

It looked like something had crawled in here, a snake for sure. He stepped up to the hole where Ray was supposed to emerge and listened. This time he thought he heard faint sounds coming from inside.

"You in there?" he hollered, instantly realizing the stupidity of his question. "How's it going?"

"It's slow and tight," Ray answered. His voice was still distant.

Eric tried not to imagine what it would be like, crawling through a sandstone hole only slightly bigger than your body.

What if you got stuck in there? he wondered. The thought was too frightening for him to consider and he was even beginning to feel a little panicked.

"It's tighter than I remembered," Ray hollered from the hole. His voice was louder now and Eric breathed a little easier.

Minutes later Ray's hands emerged from the hole followed by his outstretched arms. Then Eric could see the red hair on top of his head.

"Give me a pull," he said. "I'm tired of crawling."

Eric pulled on Ray until he dropped face down onto the cave floor.

"Whoa, what's that?" Ray was staring at the winding tracks in the sand.

"Looks like a snake," Eric said, "I was hoping you

didn't meet him inside the hole."

"Me too," Ray said, grinning.

In the weeks that followed, Eric realized that Ray was one of the bravest boys he had ever met. Ray seemed to have no fear of doing anything, except maybe confronting Keith the bully.

The cave adventure was one of many adventures Eric enjoyed with Ray and his new friends that summer. Eric especially enjoyed the hot days when the boys gathered to swim in "Lonesome Lagoon," a pool of water on Lonesome Creek, which flowed sluggishly alongside the railroad track on the south side of town.

Each afternoon a small train came lumbering down the tracks, making a low grinding noise as it sluggishly passed by. Everyone in Alexander called it "the Goose" because of the way is swayed, almost waddled down the line. The train included the engine, mail car, passenger car and usually a half-dozen box cars. A small caboose was at the end.

The track was a branch line that ran from Fairview, Montana, to Alexander and on to Watford City where the Goose would turn around and head back to Fairview. Although the 40-mile-long line was insignificant in the shipping and commerce of the Northern Plains, the Goose still played an important role in the economy of McKenzie County. The Goose transported farmers' and ranchers' cattle and wheat to market and delivered supplies and the mail.

Eric soon learned that the boys in Alexander viewed the small yellow train as *their* train; it was like a giant toy lumbering down the tracks. Occasionally they bought 25 cent passenger tickets at the Alexander station. When the train stopped at the station, they would clamber aboard, handing the surprised conductor their tickets. The boys were usually the only ones in the car.

Riding the train east through Arnegard, they watched the prairie slowly roll by, and they half closed their eyes when the train swayed and waddled across a trestle just before entering Watford City.

Watford City was literally the end of the line where the Goose threaded around a circle of tracks and then headed back west again toward Alexander, and finally to Fairview.

"I've heard there's a railroad tunnel before it gets to Fairview," Ray said one day as they watched the train pass by. "When the Goose goes through the tunnel they turn the lights on inside the passenger car so people can see."

Ray smiled at the thought. "Someday I want to ride the Goose through that tunnel; that would be a real adventure," he said. "Or if we don't do that, maybe we could hike through the tunnel on foot. That would be fun too, don't you think?

They all shook their heads in agreement. Ray was always thinking of some future adventure for them to do.

In addition to riding the Goose, the boys conducted countless experiments on the train tracks, laying pennies and nickels on the rail, along with an occasional dead prairie dog. As soon as the train passed they rushed to the tracks to examine the flattened items.

Sometimes they placed larger objects on the tracks such as rocks the size of bowling balls. As soon as the train wheels struck the rocks, they flew off the rail and bounced down the embankment.

And there were also pranks that they played on the Goose. Two brothers, Ron and Ken Berge, rigged a large net on the side of a wooden trestle crossing Lonesome Creek near their farm outside Alexander. When the train approached, the brothers stood on the trestle, facing the opposite direction, pretending not to hear the engineer's frantic blasts of the whistle. As the engine grew closer Ron and Ken jumped over the side of the trestle into their makeshift net, which instantly tore loose, dumping them into the creek below.

One afternoon when the boys swam in Lonesome Lagoon, Eric learned of yet another prank to play on the train.

"Here comes the Goose," Ray shouted to the swimmers.

They all immediately pulled their trunks to their ankles and floated bare buttocks in the water, facing the passing train. Another boy, John Hanson, who had just ridden up to the lagoon on his bike, turned so his back was facing the train, pulled down his trunks and bent over, displaying his buttocks.

"Hey John, your pants fell down," one of the boys shouted from the water.

"What a mooner!" someone added.

"I saw someone looking out the window of the mail car, I think it was a woman," Ray said. "Boy, did she look upset. *Ha, ha, ha!*"

All of the boys were laughing as they imagined the disgust on the face of the woman in the mail car and maybe others on the train.

But when Eric looked at the fleeting train, he only saw the faded yellow paint on the cars and empty windows. The Goose looked uncaring, almost tired and worn out as it waddled down the tracks. Eric glanced back at the other boys and wondered if anyone else had noticed the empty windows, but all he saw were his friends laughing and giggling in the water.

"Next time I'll do a dance for the lady in the mail car," John bragged. "She'll like that!"

Eric's first summer in Alexander was the best summer he had ever had. The hikes up to Ragged Butte, exploring the cave and the lazy afternoons at Lonesome Lagoon were all great fun. Eric thought maybe he was having all this fun because he was growing older and could do more things. Or maybe it was because he was meeting new friends.

But when Eric tried to imagine spending a summer in places like Opheim, Appam, Brockway or Lone Tree, he couldn't picture having this much fun.

On the unofficial last day of summer, the Sunday before the start of school, Eric was riding his bike to Ray's house. The day was hot for September, and the boys were gathering at Lonesome Lagoon for one last swim.

Eric was thinking of jumping into the cool lagoon when he met Anita who was riding the opposite direction. She slammed on her brakes, causing her bike to skid sideways.

"Ready for school?" she hollered as he peddled past her.

There was a pleading tone to her voice so Eric felt obliged to stop. He stopped and turned to face her. The sight of Anita standing there, holding her bike with the leather straps swaying in the breeze, brought Eric an uncomfortable feeling of having experienced this moment before.

"I guess I'm ready for school," he said.

"How's your bottom?" Anita asked.

"What?" Eric asked, his eyes widening. "What did you say?"

"I asked, how's your bottom?" Anita had a sly grin on her face.

"None of your business!" Eric shouted.

Anita was not done teasing. "Your neighbors heard you screaming," she said.

"Aw, go away, you dummy," Eric said, his face growing hot. "I'm not talking to you."

He sneered as he turned and peddled angrily away. He rode a short distance before stopping and turned to watch Anita riding in the opposite direction. Eric's face was somber and he felt his body begin to tighten.

He could almost feel those prickly, painful needles all over again.

Chapter 2

Winter

The Northern Plains have two main seasons. There's winter and there's summer, and there's not much in between. While people in other areas of the United States dwell on their lingering seasons — the greening fields of spring or the golden hills of autumn — the Northern Plains offer scant time between the two main seasons.

One day can be warm and sunny. The next can bring snow and cold. Those who live on the plains know exactly what to expect, which is the unexpected.

They even find humor in their flip-flop climate and have a favorite joke for visitors: "If you don't like the weather now, stick around for a day and it will change."

As the Anderson family entered its third year in Alexander, they were almost unaware that they were setting a record for their longevity in one place. The elevator was doing good business, so good that the company decided to leave Justin Anderson in one place for a while. The wheat and barley fields were nurtured by plentiful summer rain for three years in a row, producing bumper crops up to 30 bushels per acre, which was a good yield on the semi-arid prairie. The bumper crops generated record profits at the Alexander elevator.

As agriculture prospered, so did towns such as Alexander. The farmers and ranchers were spending more money on everything, including machinery, new cars and trucks, and expensive whiskey at the bars on Saturday nights. Along with the prosperity, however, came a growing sense of urgency. Everyone knew the good times couldn't last forever. The good times never did.

Still, a feeling of optimism was making a strange incursion into people's thinking. And a growing sense of permanence seemed to be settling on the Anderson family. They decided to fix up their house and hired Hank Olson, the town carpenter and handyman, to paint and wallpaper several rooms.

The Andersons had never done anything like this before, and they couldn't help but marvel as Hank went about his work, fixing up the place.

After several weeks, the handyman ceremoniously announced his remodeling work was done. The Andersons stood back and smiled at the freshly painted walls and wallpaper. It seemed unbelievable, but the prairie nomads were setting down roots, at least for now. For the first time, they were becoming attached to their address. Alexander was beginning to feel like a real home.

Summer ended, followed by a brief autumn, and then winter made an abrupt entrance in November. Heavy snow spread across the Northern Plains, leaving a thick, white mantle. As the winter began, it seemed that it was not as cold as most winters. But if the wind shifted to the northwest on any given day, it signaled another Canadian cold front was slipping across the border.

It was on one of those frigid days that Eric paused to look at the big thermometer outside the drug store. The mercury bar barely rose from the bottom of the thermometer.

"Thirty degrees below zero," Eric said to his sister Caroline as they stopped to look on their walk to school. Although the intense cold numbed their bodies and stung their face as they stood there, this morning's temperature still seemed unreal.

Eric remembered one afternoon in July when he had paused at this very same spot, and the thermometer read 106 degrees above zero. It was one of those mathematical mysteries of the Northern Plains. How could one place register such extremes?

Eric started to compute the temperature difference between the July and January as he and Caroline walked up the hill toward school. But the icy wind was strong that morning, and the air was so cold that it hurt to breathe. Their bodies began to ache all over from the cold, and Eric stopped computing the math. He and Caroline instinctively pulled their parka hood tighter around their faces until only their eyes were visible. Leaning into the icy wind as they walked, they could only think of the warmth awaiting them inside the school's front door.

On days like this, the teachers might grudgingly allow students to stay inside during recess and noon hour. Still, even as the boys and girls enjoyed their respite from the cold, they would look soberly out the frosted windows, dreading their walks home and wondering how much longer this frigid weather would last.

Fortunately, the spells of extreme cold, when temperatures plunged well below zero, didn't last all winter. And during moderate weather, when the mercury climbed into the 20s and 30s above zero, Eric joined his friends to go sledding on the big hill near his home. On weekends, especially, the hill was a busy place with kids pulling their sleds to the top. Their rides down the hill were fast over the packed snow, the cactus plants hibernating harmlessly somewhere below. Once the sled stopped at the bottom, the rider got off and began the long trek up the hill again.

From the top of the hill the plains stretched barren and white from horizon to horizon. On some days, the sky was bright blue, providing a sharp contrast to the snow-covered plains. On other days, the prairie wind gained strength, blasting the snow upward and blurring the horizon into subtle shades of white and gray.

On the south side of town, Lonesome Lagoon was frozen solid. The Goose still approached each day at 2 p.m., but there was no bevy of bare buttocks floating on the creek; there was only an occasional ice skater as the train passed by.

Winter changed everything in North Dakota. The prairie seemed to stand still as it entered its long winter nap. The short dreary days and long cold nights seemed to drag on with monotonous regularity. Many animals — deer, antelope, jack rabbits, coyotes and cougars — continued to roam the frozen landscape in search of food. Somehow, most of them would survive the long winter.

Others, such as prairie dogs and rattlesnakes, abandoned the earth's surface to burrow deep underground, where they lay in a dormant trance, waiting for the warming days of spring.

Humans had no choice but to continue with their lives as usual, or as closely to usual as possible. The long, bitterly cold winter affected everyone, young and old. They all wore the mask of winter on their face, a pale, somewhat tired look with a longing expression in their eyes.

Old-timers told stories of early settlers who huddled for weeks around little coal stoves in their tiny sod homes, listening to the howling winds outside and the cries of hungry coyotes and wolves. For some settlers, spring didn't come soon enough; some went mad as the cold, dreary days of winter dragged on.

One old-timer's tale was about a settler's wife who was left alone at the homestead shack as her husband drove a team of horses to the neighbors to fetch some coal. The wife put on her shawl, bonnet and white gloves. She walked out the door, never bothering to close it. When her husband returned home, he followed his wife's footsteps in the snow to a thicket of trees on the side of a hill. He found her sitting in the snow, her back against the trunk of a cottonwood tree. She looked as though she was taking one last look at the cold, dreary prairie, a slight smile frozen on her lips.

The settlers who endured the physical and mental challenges of a Dakota winter learned to console themselves with one truth: Nothing stayed constant in Dakota, and that included the weather. Just when it seemed as though winter would never end, the weather changed.

After weeks of frigid climate, the northerly winds would suddenly calm and the skies would clear. A "warm" front would slowly begin to stir to the southwest, gaining barometric pressure until it spread north across the prairie. The winds quickly increased, pushing the frigid Canadian air to the east and north and bringing air so warm it no longer hurt to breathe it.

The shifting winds were proof that the Northern Plains are a constant battleground for advancing weather fronts, both cold and warm.

It was on a mild Saturday in January, when the temperature climbed above freezing for the first time in three weeks, that Eric, Ray and John decided to hike up to Ragged Butte.

The day was calm and sunny with a bright blue sky. The winter landscape seemed to almost sparkle in the sun. As they hiked, the boys let the furry hoods of their parkas fall to their shoulders, and they took turns carrying a canvas bag filled with sandwiches, apples, three cans of pop and a flashlight. The hike seemed easy in the refreshing winter air as they climbed up the mile-long incline before reaching the coulees that led to the top of Ragged Butte.

"I can't wait to see Indian Cave," Ray said. "I wonder if it's snowed in. Maybe there are animals hibernating in there." Ray grinned at Eric and John, but their minds were elsewhere.

"Maybe we should have brought our sleds," John said as he turned to look at the long walk back to town. "We could ride our sleds part of the way back."

"I don't know if the snow is packed hard enough to sled on," Eric said.

John shrugged and they followed Ray as he climbed to the top of Ragged Butte. On the summit, the sandstone boulders provided a sharp contrast to the snow. The boys looked back toward town, which looked almost half-buried in the winter landscape. The only signs of life were plumes of smoke rising in columns from chimneys scattered throughout Alexander.

"Okay," Ray said. "Let's find the cave."

The three moved easily across the top of the butte, which had only a few inches of snow. Winter winds had blown most of the snow over the side of the butte, forming large snow banks on the eastern slope.

Ray walked to a rocky ledge and without warning jumped over the edge.

"What the heck!" John hollered. "What's he doing?"

John and Eric ran to the edge of the ledge and looked down where Ray stood, buried in snow up to his waist, the usual grin spread across his face.

"You dumb turd," John said. "You could have broke your leg or something."

"Come on," Ray said, still grinning. "Jump over; it's a soft landing in the snow."

Eric was first to move to the edge. He paused a moment and then jumped, landing a few feet from Ray.

Next came John jumping stiff as a pencil, still holding the canvas bag. "Yeeeehaaaa," he hollered as he sunk in the snow up to his chest.

Laughing, the three struggled through the deep snow until they climbed slightly up the slope, where the snow was less deep.

"It's around here somewhere," Ray said. He looked to the east, searching for the section fence in the pasture below. The section fence was a landmark to the boys because it aligned perfectly with the entrance to the cave.

Eric and John also began scanning the prairie. To the southeast rose Tub Butte, so named because it looked like a miniature volcano with a bowl-shape indentation on top. Turning to the north they could see all the way to the breaks above the Missouri River. The day was incredibly clear, with only a bank of clouds stretching across the horizon to the north of the river. The winds were still calm, even on the top of Ragged Butte. As the three looked out over the plains, the land looked as if it were still asleep in the winter sun. There was no movement, not a single jack rabbit, coyote or antelope for as far as they could see.

"There it is," Ray hollered, pointing to a faint line of posts stretching up a hillside. "We've got to go a little bit more to the north," he said.

The three moved slowly through the deep snow for several hundred feet until Ray stopped, raising his hand.

"It's down there," he said, pointing below them on the slope where a rocky ledge jutted out of the snow.

Ray climbed down to the ledge, slid around the side and stopped in the waist-high snow. I know the entrance is here!" he shouted excitedly. "I recognize this ledge."

John and Eric both slid down the slope to where Ray was. The three put their gloves on and began digging down through the snow.

"You look like a frickin' prairie dog," John said, laughing. He was pointing at Ray who was digging furiously, his head bent down, with snow flying out behind him.

"Except prairie dogs don't go out in winter," Ray laughed. "They're too smart for that. They go deep into their holes and sleep until spring."

"What are you saying, we're dumb?" John asked.

"Well, look at you," Ray said, grinning. "You're also digging with your hands in the snow on the side of Ragged Butte in the middle of January."

They all laughed and then Ray tossed a glove full of powder in John's face.

"I'll get you, you turd," John said, leaping on top of Ray. The two rolled laughing down the slope. Then they climbed back to the ledge and started digging again.

The boys' bantering and horseplay continued as they dug deeper in the snow, determined to find the entrance to the cave. Suddenly a small hole appeared in the snow bank in front of them.

"Aha, what did I tell you," Ray said. He dug more snow away from the sides and the hole grew bigger. They'd found the entrance to Indian Cave.

They scooped more snow away from the opening, and Ray slid through the hole and disappeared. John and Eric widened the hole even more and then took turns sliding into the cave. The three boys gathered at the bottom of the bank where the sandy floor of the cave began. They moved forward single file on their hands and knees until they reached the larger room.

When he stood, Eric's head brushed the ceiling. He had grown since their last visit. The cave also looked much darker than he remembered because of the snow piled across most of the entrance.

Eric was debating going back to entrance and widening the hole to let in more light when Ray reached into the canvas bag and pulled out the flashlight. He flicked it on and shined the light around the cave.

"Just checking to make sure we don't have any company in here," he said grinning. "I want to see if I can still fit in the hole in the wall."

Ray handed the flashlight to Eric and walked to a hole and leaned in. Then he pulled his head out of the hole and announced, "I'm going in."

"Are you sure?" John asked as he looked in the other hole in the wall. "It looks awfully dark in there."

"It's always dark in the hole," Ray said, sounding like a veteran cave explorer. He removed his parka and the rubber boots from covering his shoes. Then, he extended his arms up alongside his head, looking like he was about the dive into Lonesome Lagoon. Ray bent and slowly slid face down into the hole in the wall.

A familiar feeling swept over Eric as he watched Ray's body disappear into the hole. Then he heard John move behind him and he turned to face him.

"He did this before," Eric said. "It took him a long time to make it out of the other hole."

"Well I'm not in a hurry," John said, dropping the canvas bag to the floor and plopping down on the sand. Using the bag as a pillow he lay on his back and stared up at the ceiling. "It's kind of nice in here in a spooky sort of way."

Eric nodded and lay down on the floor, resting on his side, facing John. "Ray says the Indians used to put their dead people in the holes, but there's nothing in there now."

The cave was almost silent, with only faint scraping sounds coming from the hole in the wall where Ray was weaseling his way through.

Eric turned the flashlight on and moved the beam across the roof of the cave and down the other side. A faint whistling noise broke the silence and they both turned toward the cave entrance. "Breeze must be starting out there," Eric said.

The cave grew silent again, and John looked like he might fall asleep with his head propped on the canvas bag, staring blankly at the ceiling. Eric was drawing circles in the sandy floor, thinking of the Indians who probably held some sort of last rites for their dead at this very spot. The Indians probably used this cave for hundreds of years until General Custer and his cavalry arrived, chasing them onto reservations so white settlers could claim the land.

"This room has history," Eric said wistfully to John. "I can almost feel it. Can't you?"

John said nothing, only grunting to acknowledge Eric's question. Then the cave was silent again as the two boys lay on the floor.

"Eeeeeeeaaaaa!" The piercing scream came from the hole in the wall, causing both Eric and John to jump. Ray screamed again, a bloodcurdling, "eeeeeeaaa!"

Eric ran to the hole in the wall and leaned in. "You okay?" he hollered.

"Get me out of here," Ray shouted. His voice was frantic and high-pitched. "Pull me out!" he demanded.

Eric ran to the other hole, stretched his arms forward and began crawling in. He edged forward until he felt the bottoms of Ray's shoes. The space was tight and he quickly felt his claustrophobia growing. But this was no time to panic, he convinced himself, as he grabbed Ray's feet and started slowly pulling backwards.

"Come on," Eric hollered. "You've got to help!"

Eric wasn't sure if Ray even heard him, but then he felt Ray's legs begin to twist a little and slowly wriggle in the sandstone.

The air was musty and damp and it seemed hard to breathe as Eric held firmly onto Ray's shoes and tried to inch backwards. As he pulled he began to breathe harder; it felt like he was running out of air in the dark, musty hole. Eric paused for a moment, trying to catch his breath, trying not to think of the sandstone that entombed him. The rock pressed tightly on his shoulders and hips and brushed the hair on his head.

The sandstone seemed to be pressing in on him and Eric suddenly felt like screaming. His mind was racing now, on the verge of panic. He closed his eyes, lying face down on the sandstone, and tried to control his breathing.

This is too shitty. Eric thought. *Think of anything else...*

Eric remembered Clarice and her horse running across the prairie in Montana. The horse's long black tail was flowing as he galloped through the sage brush. It was a pleasing thought, and Eric felt his facial muscles trying to form a smile. His heavy breathing slowed and became almost normal again.

Suddenly he felt Ray's shoe jerk and he thought he heard a muffled scream.

Eric began pulling again on Ray's shoes, slowly wiggling in a backwards motion. He was pulling hard, but it seemed like they weren't moving. Eric felt his body growing tighter again.

We're stuck, he thought. *We're stuck in this shitty hole!*

Eric was beginning to panic. Still grasping Ray's shoes, he pulled backwards with all of his strength. He felt the sandstone slide a few inches past his shoulders and heard more muffled shouts from Ray.

Eric pulled back again on the shoes. Ray's legs began to wiggle frantically, which seemed to help. Eric arched his body against the side of the hole and pulled hard once more. He could feel the sandstone brushing past his shoulders.

"It's working!" Eric shouted in the darkness. "It's really working!"

He could hear Ray's muffled screams again as he pulled again on his shoes, moving backwards. Eric's claustrophobia suddenly vanished, replaced by his growing excitement as he thought of sliding out of the hole in the wall.

Finally, Eric could feel his feet kicking free from the hole. There was a sudden jerk as John grabbed Eric's feet and pulled hard, and Eric lost his grip on Ray's shoes.

Eric kicked his feet wildly and screamed, "Don't pull so hard! I lost Ray!"

Eric inched forward again until he felt Ray's shoes. He grabbed the shoes and began pulling again. Eric tilted his head slightly toward his feet and shouted, "Okay, pull back now!"

Slowly John pulled Eric out of the hole. Eric let loose of Ray's feet and dropped to the cave floor. Then John leaned into the hole and pulled on Ray's feet.

Ray slid out of the hole, dropping to the floor. Ray and Eric lay on the sand, breathing hard, trying to catch their breath and also calm themselves.

Ray's face looked grotesque, with his mouth open, eyes widened and his cheek bones raised high. He suddenly jerked his body away from the wall and began sliding backwards in the sand.

"There's snakes in there!" he screamed. "I felt them. I put my hand right on them!" Ray was breathing heavily, his chest heaving, and his body started to shake.

"There's snakes, a slimy pile of snakes." Ray extended his hands to Eric. "Are there any bites?"

Eric grabbed the flashlight and carefully examined Ray's trembling hands. "Nope, there's no snake bite," Eric said, trying to sound reassuring. "All you got are some scrapes from the sandstone."

Ray wiped his eyes and his gaping mouth slowly closed. John brought him his parka and rubber boots and Ray quickly put them on.

"Let's get out of here," Ray said as he began crawling back. John and Eric followed, the three crawling single file to the entrance. The three climbed out of the cave and stood there dumbfounded by the sudden change in weather. Heavy snow was falling and the wind was picking up, with sudden gusts racing across the top of Ragged Butte.

"Holy crap!" John shouted. "How can this be?"

They stood together, shocked by the sudden change in weather. The wind was growing stronger, the snow crystals stinging their faces as they pulled their parka hoods over their heads. Suddenly, much stronger wind gusts began to blast the butte.

It felt like the storm was arriving at that very moment. As the howling wind grew stronger, it began pushing the falling snow sideways across the top of Ragged Butte.

They boys were still stunned by the blizzard. They glanced at each other, wondering how this could happen so quickly.

"Come on!" Ray shouted, trying to be heard above the storm. "We've got to get going!"

The three lumbered forward into the blinding snow, feeling their way along the rocky ledge that led to the southern edge of the butte. The air was much colder now and the wind was gaining strength. The wind began to howl until it became a terrifying shrieking sound. John turned to look at Eric; they'd both heard the sound.

The boys continued trudging through the snowstorm until they reached the rocky edge of the butte. They gathered behind a large boulder to shield themselves from the strong wind.

"Okay, let's make our way down the butte," Ray said. "I'll go first."

Ray stepped out from behind the boulder and moved a few steps down the slope. He seemed to lose his balance in the wind, and he tottered then fell sideways in the snow. He lay there for a moment then climbed back up the slope to the boulder.

"Holy crap!" he shouted. "If you step out there, this frickin' blizzard will blow you right off the butte!"

The boys stared at each other through the swirling snow. The roar of the storm was deafening now, and the snow was so thick they could barely see each other. It seemed unthinkable, but the wind was still growing stronger. Eric heard the shrieking sound again, sending shivers down his back.

"We've got to go back to the cave," John shouted. "Right now!"

No one argued as they turned and began stumbling back through the blinding snow. They plunged forward, feeling their way alongside the ledge. Their movement was growing more difficult in the deepening snow, but they pushed on as fast as they could. They sensed that if they did not find their way back soon, they might never make it.

The roar of the snowstorm was growing even louder and the wind began making the screaming and shrieking sounds again. Ray turned to look back at John and Eric. Now they'd all heard the strange, terrifying sound.

By the time they reached the ledge above the cave, they were exhausted and almost out of breathe. They slid down below the ledge and began digging furiously in the snow until a small opening appeared again. Ray plunged first through the hole, followed by John and Eric. They all lay breathing heavily on the cave floor.

"Holy shit, I didn't know if we were going to make it," John said. "I've never seen a blizzard this bad. And that screaming noise in the wind, did you guys hear it?"

Eric and Ray both nodded yes as the three began crawling into the cave to the larger room. As they crawled forward, Ray glanced nervously at the walls of the cave.

When they reached the larger room they sat close to one another on the sand. John flipped on the flashlight, shining the light back toward the cave's entrance. The hole in the snow was quickly disappearing, buried by the raging storm. Still, there was some comfort as they watched the hole growing smaller. The powerful storm was sealing them in, providing them some measure of protection from the elements outside. The boys sat in silence, trying to adjust to their new surroundings.

"I wish I was home," Ray said, grabbing the flashlight and setting it in the sand so the beam shot up to the ceiling. "I wish we had never come here." His voice trailed off, sounding like it might break. His hands were trembling as he brushed snow from his parka.

They looked at one another, searching for words, but no one said anything. The growing silence inside the cave was unnerving, almost frightening compared with the deafening roar of the blizzard outside.

Sensing their growing nervousness, John cleared his throat and shook the canvas bag from his back, setting it on the floor. "Looks like we're going to spend the night here," he said. "And then maybe the storm will let up and we can hike out in the morning."

Ray glanced at the holes in the wall and slid a little closer to the flashlight. "Okay," Ray said. "Let's have our sandwiches."

They each reached in the canvas bag, removed a sandwich and a can of pop, and began to eat. The cave was growing quieter as the blizzard continued burying the entrance with more snow, blocking the roar of the storm outside.

"We're lucky we're in here," John said. "We'd be goners out there."

Eric nodded and took another bite of his sandwich. Ray seemed oblivious to their words and continued staring at the holes in the wall as he ate.

Eric noticed Ray's nervous glances at the holes. "Don't worry," Eric said. "They won't be coming out tonight."

"*How...do...you...know?*" Ray screamed the words, which echoed off the cave walls. His sudden outburst startled Eric and John.

"*How do you know?*" Ray screamed again. His voice was high-pitched and tense. It sounded like he was going to cry at any moment.

"*Because they're not!*" Eric shouted back at Ray. "*It's*

winter! Snakes never come out till spring! That's a cinch!" Eric munched hard on his sandwich to emphasis his point and took a big gulp of his soda.

Ray looked shocked, somewhat taken aback by Eric's outburst.

"He's right," John said, trying to calm things. "Those snakes are staying in the hole till spring. They know when it's the right time to come out. And now is not the right time. Snakes and winter just don't mix."

They all shook their head in agreement, even Ray. They knew a prairie rattler could kill an 800-pound steer with a single strike of its venomous fangs. But the deadly rattler could never survive one day of a Dakota winter; maybe not even an hour in the storm raging outside the cave.

Still, the boys looked uneasy, even tense as they glanced at each other. A nagging awareness was settling over them as they prepared to spend the night in the cave; they were intruding on the hibernating snakes. The boys were also aware of a paradox inside the cave. For the hibernating snakes, survival meant they must remain in the cave until spring. For the boys, survival meant they must soon leave the cave, perhaps the very next morning.

"Well, let's see here," said John, breaking the tense silence. "I think I'll have my dessert now." He reached in the bag, pulled out an apple and began chewing noisily.

"Make mine a piece of apple pie," Eric said. "I want it warm, right out of the oven." Eric laughed loudly, his voice sounding forced and exaggerated.

"Well, make mine an apple turnover," Ray said. His

voice sounded obliged and he forced a twisted grin on his frightened face.

They munched their apples and sipped their sodas, stealing occasional side glances at the cave walls and each other.

"We're lucky," John said, somberly. "We're really, really lucky."

"I hate to say this, but we should save the flashlight batteries," Eric said. "We might need the light later."

"For what?" Ray asked, his eyes widening again.

"To find our way to the entrance in the morning," Eric said.

"Oh yeah," Ray said. "We gotta walk out in the morning."

When they finished eating, they all lay down on the sand, a clump of parkas sliding closer to each other for comfort and warmth. John flicked off the flashlight.

"I guess we're kind of like the snakes right now," Eric said.

"Shut up," Ray said. "I don't want to talk about them."

"Well, anyone got a story to tell?" Eric persisted. No one responded, so he cleared his throat to speak.

"I read where there was some kind of skirmish here on Ragged Butte between the Indians and cavalry. Eventually the cavalry won and chased the Indians up to the Missouri River. When the cavalry came back to Ragged Butte several days later they found a dead chief on top of a boulder. The Indians had laid the chief out nice and formal, with a feather war bonnet on his head, beads around his neck and a tomahawk lying across his chest."

"They probably didn't have time to bring him in here," John said.

The flashlight flicked on as Ray scanned the room with the light, lingering on the empty holes in the wall.

"Let's talk about something else," Ray said. His voice was sounded strained, almost angry. He flicked the light off and they could hear him settling back on the floor.

The cave grew silent again; even the sounds of the blizzard outside were almost gone. Eric rubbed his forehead and pulled the parka hood tighter around his face.

John is right, he thought. *We're lucky to be in this cave. We're lucky to be alive.*

Eric could easily imagine the terrible blizzard still raging outside, and he began to feel a strange warmness about this place. This little cave on the side of Ragged Butte had provided solace and refuge to so many, including grieving Indians, slumbering rattlesnakes and three boys lost in a blizzard.

Their sleep that night was cold and restless. They awakened several times and stood in the dark, stomping their feet in the sand to increase circulation. Then they would lie back down in the sand and try to sleep.

The night seemed to drag on forever. When Eric awakened after what seemed like his longest snooze, the black cave seemed to have a dull lightness about it. He focused hard and could see two dark shapes lying near him. Turning, he could discern the snow-covered entrance to the cave, which had a slight transparent lightness.

"Wake up," he said, shaking the other two. "It's morning."

John and Ray mumbled and shifted in the sand, and Eric could see them turning to look at the vague light at the entrance.

"Okay," Ray said, sounding fully awake. "Let's go."

They crawled single file to the entrance and paused at the bank of snow covering the entrance. They didn't know what to expect outside the cave and were almost hesitant to start digging. Ray climbed up the bank first and John and Eric joined him, digging in the snow. It seemed like they were digging for a long time.

"That was one big blizzard to drop this much snow," John said. He grunted and scooped more snow from the bank.

Suddenly a small hole appeared, flooding the entrance with light. They dug faster, opening a hole big enough to crawl through.

One by one they emerged onto the eastern slope of Ragged Butte. The air was bitterly cold, the sky above them slate gray. The blizzard was gone, but a stiff breeze still swept across the top of the butte, carrying their breath vapors down the slope. They climbed to the top of the butte and began walking to the southern edge.

"I think we better walk west to Highway 85 and try to catch a ride," John said. His face was already flushed by the frigid air. "It's too long a hike to town the other way. And it's too cold. Way too cold ..."

They all nodded their agreement and started walking toward the highway, which crossed the summit a quarter-mile to the west. They were walking directly into the wind, which quickly numbed their faces, and then their legs and arms began to ache.

The icy air felt eerily familiar to Eric. It had the same aching coldness as the air he breathed that morning when he paused to read the thermometer outside the drug store. *It could easily be 30 below zero once again*, he thought. The blizzard and the long night in the cave had tested their will. But now they were facing their biggest test of all. This air is so cold it hurts to breathe, Eric thought. *This air is so cold it could kill us.*

The sudden realization was Eric's last fully conscious thought as the three stumbled forward into the bitterly cold wind. Their aching bodies began to shake as they were battered by the icy wind.

Their thinking deadened as they trudged forward; the only thing left was their instinct to survive. Reaching the highway, they crossed the ditch and climbed up onto the empty roadway. They impulsively turned their backs to the wind and stamped their feet on the pavement, trying to increase the circulation in their legs and lessen the pain.

The three stood like zombies on the road, with no mental capacity. Then they began walking down the long sloping highway; their eyes staring blankly ahead through the slits in their parka hoods. The town was still a long ways off, and there was no traffic to stop and help them. As they trudged down the empty highway, the pain was growing in their bodies. Then the pain mysteriously began to ease as their bodies were growing numb.

The core temperature of their bodies was dropping, their blood was thickening and their bodies were slowly abandoning the urge to warm themselves by shivering. Their body functions were beginning to shut down. They were freezing to death.

Ray suddenly stopped, pulled out his penis and pissed onto the roadway. The urine quickly froze on the pavement. He zipped up and they silently continued walking, the fur on their parka hoods buffeted by the wind.

"I'm tired," Ray said, his breath vaporizing in the wind. "I'm gonna lay down and go to sleep."

"No you're not!" John shouted. He grabbed Ray and pushed him forward. "Keep walking!"

Ray stumbled forward a few steps then stopped. "I'm going to sleep." he said, collapsing onto the roadside and curling into a fetal position.

John and Eric bent over Ray and tried to pull him back to his feet.

"You can't go to sleep!" Eric shouted. "If you go to sleep, you die!"

Ray said nothing. It looked like he was losing consciousness.

"God damn you, Ray, you're not going to sleep!" John shouted. He slapped Ray across the face and shook his shoulders. "Stay awake, damn it!"

John and Eric kneeled over Ray and tried to pick him up, but their own strength was fading in the frigid cold. They stared at one another, as though they'd reached an agreement, and then they slowly lowered Ray back onto the road. Their faces were confused and tired as they stood.

The approaching truck slammed on its brakes and slid to a stop, the front wheels coming to rest on top the frozen puddle of urine. The driver jumped from the cab and rushed toward them.

"I'll be a son of a bitch!" he shouted, a large cloud of vapor emerging from his mouth. "Are you the boys they're looking for?"

John and Eric nodded yes.

"What's wrong with your friend?" the trucker asked, motioning toward Ray who still lay on the roadside.

"He's freezing," John said, almost in a whisper.

The trucker took the three boys to Ray's house. His parents hugged all three boys as they stumbled into the house. Eric noticed a single tear sliding down the cheek of Ray's mother.

"Thank God you're alive," she said. Ray's mother stepped back slightly to get a better look at the boys. She opened her mouth as if to speak but no words came out. There was only a low sobbing noise as she burst into tears.

Minutes later, Eric and John's parents arrived, rushing into the house. There were more hugs and tears, and then they called Vivian Erickson, a nurse who lived in Alexander. Vivian arrived minutes later and examined the boys; she said Ray should be taken to the hospital in Williston to be treated for his hypothermia. She said Eric and John, however, could recover at home.

"Keep them warm," the nurse instructed Eric and John's parents. "If they still feel chilled, you can wrap them in a blanket, but the main thing is to keep them warm. If they're hungry, give them lots of snacks, which will provide them energy and that will help warm their bodies."

She paused for a moment so they could absorb her instructions.

"They can drink warm liquids," she continued, "but don't give them hot liquids."

When Eric parents took him home his mother removed his clothing, wrapped him a quilt and put him in his bed. As the day progressed and Eric's body continued to warm, his thought processes began to clear.

By late afternoon, Eric still lay in bed, drinking a mug of warm cocoa. He stretched his legs until he felt Tiny at the foot of his bed. Tiny's legs were moving and his ears twitching, a sure sign he was dreaming again.

Eric laughed a little at his dog and then his face turned somber again. He was thinking about the blizzard, the cold night on the cave floor and the numbing walk through the biting cold.

We were lucky, he thought. *If that trucker hadn't come when he did …*

Eric shook his head at the wonder of their survival. He glanced toward the window, where bright sunlight was now shining into his room. The sunlight looked warm and inviting, but Eric sensed it was still bitterly cold outside, probably far below zero. The prairie in winter could be so deceiving and dangerous too.

And like so many things on the prairie, their hike up to Ragged Butte had such a pleasing beginning and harrowing ending. At first there was only the beautiful winter morning, the blue sky and the crystal white snow, sparkling in the sun.

It was hard to imagine such a pleasant part of that day existed, but it really did.

And then the blizzard suddenly struck, forcing them back into the cave. Still, it had seemed they were safe until they emerged the next morning into the frigid air — air so cold it hurt to breathe, air so cold it could kill you.

Eric would never forget their painful hike: Ray mumbling incoherently and stopping to piss onto the highway, his urine instantly freezing on the pavement, the terrible aching feeling in their bodies. And the air was so unbelievably cold.

But when Eric thought of all the misery they endured, there was one thought that kept rushing back. It disturbed Eric to even think of it.

He shuddered, even as he lay there in his warm bed, remembering the moment when he and John struggled to lift Ray up from the pavement. Their strength seemed to vanish as they looked at each other above Ray's slumping body, and then they laid Ray back down.

We were going to leave him there, Eric thought. *We were going to leave Ray there to die.*

Chapter 3

The Galloping Goose

The long, cold winter ended abruptly one sunny day in March. A surprising warm wind suddenly blew in from the southwest, gaining strength as the day progressed. By midafternoon a full gale was blasting the prairie and quickly melting the snow.

Small creeks formed in the coulees leading down from the buttes around Alexander. The creeks flowed down the slopes and converged in Andre Eikren's pasture on the west side of town. The snowmelt then flowed into a large drainage ditch that ran south, channeling the spring runoff through town and emptying into Lonesome Creek.

Townspeople gathered on the small wooden bridges that crossed the runoff channel to watch the water flow by. Spring runoff was the one time of the year when water was everywhere on the prairie, a fleeting moment and a spectacle to be watched by everyone.

As the snow disappeared, the farmers and ranchers began making plans for their spring planting. The days were growing warmer and the prairie was coming to life, nurtured by the sunny days that were followed by spring showers and an occasional wet spring snowfall.

The prairie began to turn emerald green. The land suddenly looked lush and fertile where only weeks before it lay frozen and covered with the dirty white snow of late winter.

The plains people were also transformed at this time of the year. The winter gloom vanished from their faces. They began to smile with happy thoughts of spring and the coming summer.

As summer vacation began, Eric and his friends often spent their days on their bicycles, riding in small groups out of town into the surrounding countryside. The boys were now 12 years old, and as their legs grew longer so did the distances they rode into the country.

On this day, Eric, Ray and John pedaled their bikes out of Alexander on a narrow dirt road heading west toward the tiny town of Cartwright. They planned to go swimming in Charbonneau Creek and then explore the nearby railroad tunnel. They followed the road up a slight rise near Larson's Butte and then descended onto a broad plain. The prairie grass was knee-high and still dark green from the spring rains.

The day was sunny and warm. John and Ray were up front and as they rode, with Eric following, deep in his own thoughts. Eric stopped and turned to look back at the landscape as he straddled his bike. He could see Ragged Butte rising above the sloping prairie to the east. For Eric, the nagging memories remained of that nearly fatal winter day. He shook his head as he remembered the frigid wind, his aching legs and the icy air so bitterly cold it hurt to breathe it.

Eric stood transfixed by the view — the yellow sandstone boulders on top Ragged Butte rising above the lush, green prairie. The sky was an incredible blue, and Eric heard a meadowlark singing somewhere off in the distance.

The prairie looked so warm, inviting and peaceful. And above it all stood Ragged Butte, where only five months earlier they nearly froze to death.

Eric slowly shook his head as he thought of the enormous differences between winter and summer on the plains. He knew that seasonal changes came as the Earth tilted on its axis; they'd learned that when they studied climate in school. But what Eric couldn't understand were the extremes in temperature, especially here in Dakota.

On this day, the prairie was warm and inviting, even beautiful. But on that winter day five months ago, this same prairie was a terrifying and lifeless landscape covered by swirling snow below a slate gray sky. And the air, the air so bitterly cold it hurt to breathe. The air so cold it nearly killed them.

Eric glanced one last time at Ragged Butte, then turned and pushed off, pedaling his bike fast to catch up with the others.

"Hey, look at that!" Ray was pointing to the south. They stopped and shaded their eyes and spotted the antelope. There were five of them grazing not far from the dirt road. When the antelope heard Ray shout they stopped grazing and raised their heads to stare back at the boys.

"Hey, watch this," Ray said. He dropped his bicycle and lay on the ground, his feet sticking straight up in the air.

Ray began to make strange, silly sounds. "Eeeha! Eeeeehaaa! Geeedahhh!"

He was motioning with his hand toward the antelope. John and Eric turned to look at the antelope, which were moving closer.

"They're curious," Ray said, still lying on the ground. "Get down here, you guys. Do what I'm doing and I bet we can get them to walk right up to us."

John and Eric dropped their bikes and lay down on the ground, mimicking Ray, making strange sounds and kicking their legs in the air.

The antelope continued their cautious approach until they stood just a few feet from the boys, staring down at them.

Eric had never been this close to an antelope in the wild. He was a surprised by the intense curious look in their eyes as they sniffed the air, staring down at them. The antelope looked strange up so close, with their brown and white coats and their distinct horns. They looked exotic, reminding Eric of the African antelope he'd seen in movies.

"Boo!" Ray suddenly shouted at the antelope, waving his hand at them. "If this were hunting season, you'd all be dead."

The antelope instantly jumped sideways and ran away. The boys stood laughing at the fleeing antelope, which were moving with incredible speed.

"Curiosity could kill those antelope," Ray said. "They shouldn't approach a human. If this was October, they'd be dead."

"That's what I was thinking," Eric added. "They won't

last long in hunting season if they stay that curious."

The three got on their bikes and continued west until they reached Cartwright. The small dirt road widened a bit as it entered town near the grain elevator. They rode past the elevator and turned onto a smaller dirt trail leading to Charbonneau Creek.

Charbonneau Creek was a typical meandering prairie stream. The creek flowed west past Cartwright near the railroad tracks. There were numerous springs that emptied into Charbonneau Creek, making it a much clearer than most streams on the prairie.

The boys rode their bikes along the dirt road, which soon turned away from the rail line and followed the creek. They were getting closer to their favorite swimming hole.

Up ahead they could see the creek flowing to the base of a tall hill and then winding around the side. Although they couldn't see the confluence from where they stood, they knew Charbonneau Creek emptied into the Yellowstone River, somewhere on the other side of the hill.

Occasionally when the boys came here they would see a lone fisherman casting his line into the clear water, but usually there was no one. The boys therefore considered the Charbonneau Creek and the nearby railroad tunnel as *their* special spot, one more hidden place on the prairie for only them to enjoy.

They rode their bikes to the familiar grassy spot, then stopped and stripped off their clothes. Ray was first to jump off the bank into the pool of water, followed by John and Eric. The water was cold and clear.

Eric dropped under the surface and opened his eyes. He could clearly see Ray and John treading water nearby, their legs moving forward and back. Eric swam up to the surface, took a big gulp of air, and then dived back down to the bottom of the shallow stream. He picked up a bright red rock from the bottom then swam back up.

After breaking the surface he held the rock in the air so Ray and John could see it. "Found this on the bottom," Eric said. "Boy is this water clear!"

Ray and John both dove underwater to begin their own searches. Eric swam to shore, walked to the grassy spot and sat down on his shirt, examining the rock closer.

A sudden gust of wind moved through the cottonwood trees lining the other side of the creek; the leaves began to tremble, producing a shimmering sound. Eric sat still, listening to the unique fluttering noise of the cottonwood. It was the familiar sound of summer on the plains, and it came only from this tree.

He lay on his back on the grass, staring lazily up at the cloudless sky. Warm air flowed over his body, quickly drying his skin.

It felt really good to be here with Ray and John, enjoying the clear, cool waters of Charbonneau Creek, listening to the cottonwoods and lying in the sun.

"Okay, let's go in the railroad tunnel," Ray said as he and John approached. Water was dripping from their bodies and they both shook their heads to dry their hair. They dressed and laced their shoes.

"We should leave the bikes here," Ray said. "The tunnel is just a little ways from here."

"What about our lunch sacks?" Eric asked. "If we leave them here the gophers will eat our lunch."

"Not if we put them in this canvas sack and hoist it up into the tree," Ray said. He pulled a sack and thin rope from the bag on the side of his bike. They all put their lunches in the sack, tossed the rope over a tree branch and hoisted the sack upward.

"Okay, let's go," John said.

They followed a narrow trail that led into a wall of tall, thick brush. They began pushing forward through the brush, the small branches scraping their arms and legs as they moved. Then suddenly the brush ended and they stepped onto the side of the railroad tracks. The tracks ran straight into the nearby tunnel, a black hole in the hillside framed by thick wooden timbers.

The tunnel, less than one-quarter mile in length, was the only railroad tunnel in North Dakota. At the other end of the tunnel, on the other side of hill, the railroad tracks continued onto Fairview Bridge, which spanned the Yellowstone River.

The rail line was the exclusive domain of the Goose, and the Goose, of course, was considered by the boys to be *their* train.

The train, which some called the Galloping Goose because of the way it swayed, almost waddled down the line, traversed these tracks twice a day. The boys had never seen it happen, but they knew the Goose would emerge from this tunnel each day as it headed east. The Goose would continue east for 40 miles to Watford City and then it would loop around and begin heading back.

By late afternoon the Goose would pass this point again, going in the opposite direction. The boys examined the tunnel entrance, imagining their Goose pulling a line of cars into the tunnel until the caboose passed by, disappearing into the darkness.

The entrance to the railroad tunnel was almost hidden by the tall cottonwood trees lining the nearby creek. Because of the camouflage, the tunnel was mostly unnoticed or ignored, even by local residents. Therefore, the boys laid claim to one more piece of the prairie, a dark railroad tunnel in a hillside near Charbonneau Creek.

"This is our tunnel," Ray proclaimed as the three cautiously entered, following the tracks. The farther they went into the tunnel, the darker it got. They heard flapping noises above them.

"What is that, birds?" John asked.

"Bats," Ray answered. "There are probably hundreds of them living in this tunnel."

Eric heard a sudden scraping sound behind him and a loud thud.

"Shit," John said. "I tripped on the damn rail. It's dark in here!"

"Shut up and keep walking," Ray said. Eric heard Ray chuckle as they moved forward, Ray leading the way as usual.

"You shut up," John said. "I scraped my knee and I think it's bleeding."

They walked in silence; the only sounds were their feet shuffling on the track bed and an occasional bat flapping overhead. Toward the middle of the tunnel it became so dark they couldn't see each other. Ray stumbled and fell, and a sudden thud echoed on the tunnel walls.

"Ouch!" he shouted. "Darn it!" Eric and John stood still in the dark so they wouldn't step on him. They didn't move until they heard Ray pick himself up.

"Shut up and keep walking," John said.

There was silence for a moment, and then they all began to laugh, even Ray. Their voices echoed through the darkness.

As they moved forward they could see a small lighted area ahead, the tunnel's western entrance. As they neared the entrance, the darkness faded and in a few minutes they emerged from the tunnel into the bright sun. They stood on the tracks, holding their hands above their eyes as they adjusted to the sudden bright light.

The railroad tracks ran straight forward onto Fairview Bridge, and now they could see the muddy Yellowstone River below.

The metal-frame bridge was an impressive sight, with two large towers in the middle. It was painted black and had a daunting look as it stretched across the Yellowstone.

"This bridge was built around 1912," Ray said, suddenly sounding like a tour guide. "Great Northern Railroad built the bridge to expand its rail lines into eastern Montana." As they walked onto the bridge they looked up at the two towers anchoring the center of the span. "This was a lift bridge," Ray continued. "The two towers are 100 feet tall and they were used to raise part of the bridge should a river boat approach to pass underneath."

"Yeah, we already knew that," John said sarcastically.

"Yes, but did you know they raised the center part of the bridge only one time, shortly after they finished building the bridge?" Ray continued. "I guess they were testing it to see if the lift worked. Anyway, it was never lifted again."

John and Eric glanced at each other and smirked. They knew Ray liked to have the last word.

Pausing in the center of the bridge, they looked over the side railing and down at the muddy Yellowstone River; the water was churning and moving very fast, fed by the spring thaw in the mountains hundreds of miles to the west.

"Okay, let's climb to the top of the towers," Ray said, motioning to the other two.

"I'm not going up there," John said.

"Me neither," Eric said.

"Chickenshits, chickenshits," Ray teased. "Ah, chicken, chicken, chickenshits."

When he saw the embarrassed anger growing on their faces, Ray stopped taunting them and climbed onto the rail. Then he stepped onto a narrow ladder, which went up the side of the bridge to the top of the tower.

Ray was not particularly graceful as he climbed upward, but he had a steady, determined movement. Eric and John stood on the bridge deck, their heads tilted fully back as they watched Ray climb to the top.

"Boy I'm glad that's not me," John said. He glanced at Eric, expecting a response.

"Oh, what the heck," Eric said. "I'm going up there too."

Somewhat bewildered, John stood alone on the bridge, watching Eric climb onto the railing then step onto the narrow ladder. Eric looked straight ahead and began methodically climbing one rung at a time, slowly moving up the ladder. When he thought he was about halfway to the top, he stopped to look up for the first time. He could see Ray's head peering over the edge at the top of tower, watching Eric climb. It looked like Ray was lying flat on his stomach.

A sudden gust of wind swept across the bridge, and Eric thought he heard a creaking noise, but he wasn't sure. He looked down to see how far he had climbed. He could see John standing on the deck of the bridge, looking very small as he waved up at him. Everything seemed to take on a different dimension from this height. The deck of the bridge suddenly looked a long ways down, and even farther below the deck was the river. Eric stared down at the muddy, churning Yellowstone, which seemed oblivious to the bridge and the boys on it.

Everything around him suddenly looked different. Eric felt like he was shrinking into a small figure on a ladder on a very large bridge, high above the Yellowstone. A tight, anxious feeling was growing in Eric's stomach. The fear seemed to come rushing down on him all at once, and he began to feel light headed. He could feel his arms and legs tighten as he clung to the ladder. His breathing suddenly grew heavier and more rapid.

Eric was starting to panic. He stood frozen on the ladder, feeling as though he was suspended in air, with nothing holding him. There was only the sky above and river below.

Another gust of wind buffeted Eric's side and he felt his legs begin to shake. The tightness was growing in his stomach and Eric felt like he might throw up.

An acrid taste filled his mouth and he turned his head from the ladder to spit the pungent taste.

Eric carefully moved one foot down to the next rung. He took a deep breath and lowered his other foot, simultaneously sliding his hands down the ladder. Then he cautiously repeated this motion.

His nausea seemed to lessen as he moved. He took a deep breath and lowered himself down one more rung. *Step by step*, he thought.

The ladder rungs continued to pass by, with Eric looking straight ahead as he continued his descent.

His arms and legs began to ache, and the tightness in his stomach was growing worse. *Just keep climbing down,* he thought.

As he lowered his foot to the next rung, his foot suddenly banged against something. He glanced down to see he had reached the railing on the bridge. He heard footsteps approaching.

"What's the matter?" John asked. "Did you get scared? Did you give up?"

Eric ignored John's questions, focusing only on the railing. This was the tricky part of the climb where Eric had to swing from the ladder around the railing and drop down onto the bridge deck. Normally this would have been an easy move, but Eric knew his body was now gripped by fear. The aching pain in his arms and legs was getting worse, and his body was starting to shake. Eric's heart was pounding now, and the acrid taste filled his mouth again. He abruptly swung around from the ladder and dropped onto the bridge deck.

Eric immediately stumbled to the railing, leaned over and vomited. He watched his heave fall to the river, splattering onto the muddy surface and quickly disappearing in the current.

Eric's body began shaking and he turned away from the railing, falling to his side on the deck.

He vomited again onto the deck, making a loud heaving noise that echoed across the bridge. Eric crawled backwards on his hand and knees, vomiting again and then again.

The heaving continued until there was nothing left inside him. Eric lay gasping on his side, his face white and covered with sweat. He glanced up as John approached then lowered his head again, staring at the deck.

"Holly crap!" John exclaimed. "Are you okay?"

Eric shook his head. Still breathing heavily, he raised his right arm but then dropped it to the deck.

They stared at each other in silence until Eric had the strength to speak.

"I got scared," he said in a hushed voice. "I got really scared."

Eric's breathing was still heavy as he stared down at

the deck again. Loud wrenching dry heaves suddenly wracked his body. Then the dry heaves suddenly stopped and Eric seemed to calm a little. He took a deep breath before speaking.

"When I was on the ladder, I looked up at Ray and then I looked down at you. And when I looked down, I saw how far it was to the water and that scared the shit out of me. I freaked, I really freaked."

John laughed, but for only an instant. He abruptly stopped when he saw the pained look on Eric's face.

"Okay, let's get off this frickin' bridge," John said. "Did you hear it creaking in the wind? This bridge is starting to give me the willies."

Eric stood slowly, brushed some vomit from the side of his pants and they began walking. When they reached the end of the bridge Eric went to sit on a pile of wooden timbers alongside the tracks near the tunnel entrance.

"Should we wait here for Ray?" John asked "Or should we go back through the tunnel?"

"Let's wait for him," Eric said as he turned and spit in the dirt.

Soon they could see Ray climbing onto the ladder at the top of the tower. He moved steadily down the ladder, his shirt tails blowing in the wind. Reaching the railing, he swung around, dropping onto the deck and began walking toward them.

"So what happened to you, Eric?" Ray shouted.

"I freaked," Eric said. "That's all I can say."

Ray shrugged and turned to look back at the tower.

"It was really neat at the top," he said. "It was like I could see half of North Dakota from up there and half of Montana too."

"Didn't you get a little queasy climbing up?" Eric asked.

"Nope," Ray said.

"Well I'm hungry," John said. "So let's head back to the swimming hole and eat our sandwiches."

They all nodded their agreement and walked into the tunnel. The cool, dark air felt welcome to Eric as they moved forward. There was only the sound of their feet on track bed and an occasional bat flapping overhead.

"Damn bats," Ray said. "I don't want them to fly down and get tangled in my hair."

"They don't do that," John sneered. "That's an old wives' tale."

"They do too," Ray said. "I read it in Reader's Digest." Once again Ray had the last word.

As they continued walking into the tunnel it soon became dark. They occasionally stopped and brushed their feet along the rail to guide them as they moved forward.

The silence seemed to be growing as they neared the middle of the tunnel, not even the bats were moving overhead. Soon they could see a small light, far ahead of them at the other end of the tunnel.

Then they heard the train whistle, a low moaning sound that was almost lost in the darkness.

"Mmmmmooooooooooaaaaahhhhh."

They all froze, their ears turned toward the sound, unsure if they really heard it. Then the whistle sounded again.

"Mmmmmoooooooooaaaaahhhhh."

"Shit, it's the Goose!" John screamed. "It's coming!"

They all began scrambling forward in the darkness. But they only moved a few steps before John stumbled, falling to the ground. Ray and Eric toppled over him and slid forward on the gravel.

"Shit," Ray said as they all picked themselves up.

"Mmmmmoooooooooaaaaahhhhh."

The train horn seemed to be growing louder.

They began running full speed in the darkness, the only sounds were their shoes pounding on the track bed.

As they ran, John suddenly screamed, a piercing high-pitched shriek that echoed off the walls. "We're going to die!" he shouted; then he screamed again, a blood-curdling sound that filled the tunnel.

The sounds of their breathing and pounding feet seemed in perfect unison, one frenzied movement, as they ran toward the end of the tunnel.

"Mmmmmoooooooooaaaaahhhhh."

"Don't look back! " Ray screamed. "Just keep running!"

As they approached the entrance the darkness was beginning to fade. They could clearly see the track bed, and they picked up their speed, a final burst to the finish.

"Mmmmmoooooooooaaaaahhhhh."

It sounded like the train was right behind them, bearing down on them, about to crush them on the tracks.

The three emerged side by side from the tunnel. They ran in perfect unison, and then turned off the tracks, throwing themselves down the embankment. They rolled down the bank in a cloud of dust and then stopped as they rolled against the bushes.

Gasping for air, the three lay on the bank staring back at the tunnel, expecting to see the Goose emerge at any second.

"Holy shit," John said, almost crying. "I thought we were going to die in there."

Ray and Eric nodded. The three lay motionless in the brush, looking straight ahead.

Minutes passed and still there was no Goose. They stood and examined their bodies. Ray's pants were torn at the knees, and blood oozed from one knee. John's pants were ripped down one side and his chin was bruised.

Eric had a bruise on his forehead, and one knee was bleeding through a tear in his pants. The other pant leg was still covered in vomit, which was beginning to dry.

"Well, where is it?" John asked. He almost sounded upset.

"Mmmmmooooooooooaaaaahhhhh."

They cautiously moved closer to the tracks so they could see back into the tunnel.

"Mmmmmooooooooooaaaaahhhhh."

Dozens of bats suddenly flew out of the top of the

tunnel and scattered into the nearby cottonwoods.

The Goose emerged from the tunnel, swaying and waddling, almost in slow motion. There was a low grinding noise as it sluggishly passed by. The engineer, his elbow resting on the open window, stared down at the boys as he passed. He didn't wave, but he sounded the horn twice, apparently as a greeting.

"Mmmmmooooooooooaaaaahhhhh.

Mmmmmooooooooooaaaaahhhhh."

The passing train included the engine, mail car, passenger car, three box cars and the caboose. The boys stared in disbelief as the Goose waddled its way down the tracks. The train, *their* train, suddenly didn't look very threatening at all.

"Shit," John said. "We could have walked out the tunnel."

As the Goose continued moving down the tracks, the boys turned to look at each other again and examined their cuts and bruises more closely. John made a face when he looked at the vomit on Eric's leg.

"Hell, we could have crawled out of the tunnel and still beat the Goose," Ray said, a grin forming on his face.

"We almost did," John said.

They all began to laugh as they stood alongside the empty tracks.

"We sure beat the hell out of ourselves getting out of the tunnel," John said. "What a waste."

Their laughter grew louder as they fell to the ground,

holding their sides.

"And I puked all over the damn bridge," Eric boasted.

Their laughed so hard they began rocking back and forth on the ground. They rolled forward and back in the dirt, laughing at their frenzied run through the tunnel. It felt really good to laugh at themselves. Although none of them would admit it, it also felt good to be alive.

They picked themselves up and stepped into the brush and began making their way back to Charbonneau Creek.

Arriving at their swimming hole, the three stripped and jumped in the water. Eric swam underwater, opening his mouth to try to wash the acrid taste away.

After the swim, the three sat on the bank eating their sandwiches.

"Boy, was I hungry," Ray said. "There's nothing like running through a tunnel, chased by the Goose, to get your appetite going."

They laughed again and finished eating their lunches. The boys spent the rest of the afternoon swimming in Charbonneau Creek. They also explored the banks along the creek, looking for water snakes and frogs.

The sun was beginning to lower in the western sky when they decided they'd better head for home.

They rode their bicycles at a steady pace down the dirt road toward Alexander. The sun was slowly dropping in the west behind them, and although none of them would admit it, none of them wanted to be riding their bikes across the prairie at night. They rode into Alexander just as dusk began, and the three parted to go to their homes.

Eric rode up to his house, dropped his bike on the grass and rushed inside the house. He was hungry after the long bike ride and anxious to have supper.

"Where have you been?" his dad asked when he walked in the door. "And what happened to you?' He was looking at the bruise on Eric's forehead, his torn pants and the vomit on his pant leg.

"I had accident on my bike" Eric said, trying to keep an honest face. "We went riding out past Larson's Butte and before we knew it the sun was almost setting." He turned to face his mother, who was staring at the vomit stain on his pants. "And I threw up after my bike accident," he said.

His mother dished him a plate of macaroni hot dish and poured him a big glass of milk as he sat down at the table.

She had a suspicious look in her eyes as she examined the bruise on Eric's forehead and the cut on his knee.

"You're a mess," she said. "After you eat, take a shower and I'll bandage your cut.

Eric's bed felt welcome that night. They had ridden their bicycles a long ways, much longer than their parents would have allowed had they known the boys' plans. Tiny walked into his room and jumped up onto the foot of the bed. Eric moved his foot under the covers against Tiny's back, giving him a little rub.

He began to think of all the things they had done. The

swim in the cool, clear water of Charbonneau Creek was especially nice. Eric had never seen the water so pure that you could open your eyes and see what was around you.

Then he shuddered when he remembered the fear that suddenly enveloped him while he clung to the ladder on Fairview Bridge, high above the Yellowstone. It was such a long ways down to the churning, brown water.

And then their frantic run through the railroad tunnel, fleeing from the Goose, which unbeknown to them was still far behind them, waddling slowly down the tracks.

Eric laughed a little, but then his face turned somber.

His parents might have a hard time believing he did all these things in one day. But it didn't matter because Eric hadn't told them the truth. His parents knew nothing of what he had had done that day. He had lied to them both while keeping a perfectly straight face.

Eric would remember the day's adventures for a long time, but he would also remember his own deceit, and that would cast a pall over everything.

Chapter 4

Moonlight

Eric had wanted a horse for a long time, ever since his older sister Clarice was given a horse for her 10th birthday.

Clarice's horse was a feisty stallion with a black coat and shiny dark eyes. His name was Duke, and he had a haughty temperament to match his name.

There were two things that Duke hated. The number one thing that Duke hated was strangers, especially when they climbed up on his back and tried to ride him. And number two, Duke hated fences, perhaps as much as he hated strangers.

Clarice's horse stood tall and muscular, formidable in appearance. Duke's dark coat made him stand out even more, and the mane on his neck was thick and stiff. The stallion held his head high, always appearing to be looking down on his surroundings.

The big stallion seemed like a strange birthday gift to be given a girl, but when Clarice first climbed up on Duke's back, there was some sort of instant connection between the two. The girl and her horse looked like they belonged together.

Still, it was a strange sight, seeing the girl sitting on top her big stallion. Sometimes Eric and Caroline rode bareback behind their older sister, but even the three of them still looked very small on top the giant horse.

The Andersons were living in Brockway, a dusty little town with weathered houses scattered next to the railroad tracks on the plains of eastern Montana. Justin Anderson was managing the Brockway elevator. The town was surrounded by low, rolling hills where huge ranches stretched for miles and there were few people. In this part of Montana, much of the land remained native grassland, with no fences separating the ranches. Livestock roamed free across the prairie with only the brands on their rumps to link them to their owners.

They called this land "open range," and it stretched from horizon to horizon under the big sky. This was cattle and cowboy country, and it seemed only natural that the Anderson family should have at least one horse. When Clarice's 10th birthday approached, her parents bought Duke from a local rancher. There was a small pasture behind the Andersons' house where Duke would stay. On the first day that Clarice led Duke into the pasture he seemed to notice every detail, pausing to sniff the fence and the rusting wire. Clarice thought he was just familiarizing himself with his new home, but Duke had other things in mind.

In the days that followed, Clarice went to the pasture each morning, gave her horse a hug and with the help of her mother she saddled up. Clarice spent the entire day with Duke, riding across the open range and grooming him when they got home. As each day neared an end,

Clarice would feed Duke a pail of oats and she'd spread fresh hay for him to eat. Then she went into the house for supper.

Clarice and Duke spent that summer riding far out on to the range, exploring the hills and coulees. Sometimes she encouraged Duke to gingerly walk over the top of prairie dog towns. When a prairie dog ducked into a hole, Duke would go to the hole and sniff it; sometimes he would stomp the ground with his front hoofs as though attempting to bring the prairie dog back to the surface.

They had another game. If they saw deer or antelope, Clarice would tap her heels on Duke's sides and he'd break into a full gallop, chasing the creatures. Duke would run after them up the coulees and over the hills, with Claire whooping and laughing on his back.

The semi-arid climate in this part of Montana offered mostly dry days, but occasionally Clarice and Duke would get caught in a drenching thunderstorm. Then they would head for home, sloshing through the mud. When they got home a pail of dry oats awaited Duke, but for Clarice there was only a scolding from her mother.

Still, Clarice and Duke remained oblivious to the forces of nature; it was as if there was nothing that could stop them from going anywhere they wanted. Duke, especially, was a very happy horse. As they rode across the prairie, there was not a fence in sight.

But still, Duke had the darker side. If anyone other than Clarice and her siblings climbed on top of him, Duke became agitated. His eyes would suddenly darken and he'd nervously pace the ground. Then he'd launch himself into a frenzied bucking spree.

Duke would leap high in the air, arching his back, and when his feet returned to the ground, he'd twist his body in sudden violent moves, and then he's buck high in the air again. In just a few moments the unwelcome rider would fly through the air and crash into the ground.

The only people Duke tolerated on his back were Clarice, Caroline and Eric. If anyone else climbed onto his back Duke bucked them off.

Even Clarice's father, Justin, was not welcome. He decided to go for a little ride one morning before heading to work. But as soon as he swung up into the saddle, Duke's ears flattened and his eyes flashed darker and then he suddenly launched into his bucking routine. Justin flew out of the saddle and landed hard in some sage brush nearby. He lay stunned on the ground, then picked himself up and brushed the dust from his pants. He walked angrily to Duke and grabbed his bridle so he could look straight in the stallion's eyes.

"You're not worth the hay we feed you!" he shouted.

Duke snorted and pulled his head up, stepping back from Justin. Clarice said nothing as she watched her father angrily walk to his pickup truck and drive off to work.

———

Two days later, a cowboy arrived at the Anderson home to tame Clarice's misbehaving stallion; he had been hired by Clarice's father. The cowboy's name was Jake Olson, and he occasionally worked as a horse trainer. Jake was a wiry, tough-looking man with a weathered face. He looked like he'd been working on the range for a long time.

"Where is he?" Jake asked as he got out of his pickup truck. Clarice pointed to the pasture behind the house. Jake nodded as he removed his billfold and a can of chewing tobacco from his pockets, placing them on the seat in his truck. Then he walked with Clarice to the pasture, where Eric and Caroline were waiting to watch the trainer at work.

"Here he is," Clarice said as they stepped into the pasture. She already had Duke saddled up.

Jake adjusted the stirrups to his liking and swung up onto Duke's back, tightening his legs and pulling back on the reins, forcing Duke to hold his head high. It looked like this cowboy knew exactly what to do.

"Whoa boy," he said as Duke shifted his feet and pawed the ground. "Whoa, settle down boy."

Duke's eyes looked stunned and confused as he continued pacing back and forth.

"Okay, boy," the trainer said in a firm voice. "Let's go once around the pasture." The trainer tapped his heels on Duke's sides, motioning for him to go forward.

Duke instantly started to buck, leaping high off the ground, his back arched upward. As Duke's feet returned to the ground he twisted his body in sudden jerking motions, before bucking high once again.

On the second buck the cowboy flew sideways out of the saddle, landing hard on the ground and sliding forward on his belly. He lay still for a moment, apparently dazed, before picking himself up.

"Whoa, that was a surprise," he said, shaking his head and brushing the dust from his clothing. "I didn't know that was coming. He's a wild one all right,"

For the next 40 minutes the trainer tried unsuccessfully to ride Duke. But each time he climbed up into the saddle, Duke bucked him out.

"Okay, boy, let's try that again," the cowboy said each time before he mounted the horse. As soon as the cowboy settled in the saddle Duke would launch into frenzied bucking, jumping high off the ground, arching his back even higher, and twisting sharply as soon as his feet reached the ground.

"Okay, boy, one more time," Jake said as he swung up into the saddle. He was holding the reins even tighter this time and it looked like his legs were glued to the sides of the horse.

Duke suddenly kicked his rear legs up in the air and lowered his head; the cowboy flew forward over Duke's head and smashed into the ground, sliding to stop in a cloud of dust.

Jake lay still on the ground. Clarice was about to run into the pasture to see if he was all right when Jake began to move and slowly picked himself up. He brushed the dirt from his clothes and shook his head as he looked at Duke.

"I don't know," he said. "Some horses just can't be broke of their bad habits. He might be one of them."

They noticed Jake had a slight limp as he walked to his pickup. He started the pickup and rolled down the window, sticking his head out.

"Tell your old man there's no charge," he hollered.

The cowboy waved goodbye and drove off.

"Well, so much for that," Caroline said, shrugging as she turned for the house.

"I guess so," Clarice agreed. There was a worried look on her face. It was clear that Duke was a very stubborn horse and now Clarice wondered what fate Duke's stubborn nature might bring him.

Duke soon became the talk of the town. When the ranchers and cowboys gathered in the Silver Dollar tavern on Saturday nights they'd gossip about the "town girl's horse" that bucked everyone else off, even Jake Olson.

But Duke's wild, bucking routine was just one of his bad habits, the Andersons soon discovered.

As summer neared its end, Clarice started getting ready for school. This meant she had less time to ride her horse. Duke grew restless and bored in his pasture, and he began to examine the fence. The weathered posts and rusting barbed wire were the only things keeping him in, and when Duke looked out over the fence, he saw nothing but rolling prairie.

One day Clarice, Caroline and Eric went with their mother to the nearby town of Jordan to buy clothes for school. When they returned home, the pasture was empty.

"Oh, my God," Clarice said. "Where's Duke?" She

quickly walked around the pasture, looking for clues until she spotted the fence post leaning toward the ground.

"Oh, no!" Clarice shouted. "I think Duke jumped the fence."

Moments later, their father arrived in his pickup, picked up Clarice and Eric, and they drove out onto the open range. They didn't know which direction to go, so they drove to the south where Clarice and Duke often rode. As they drove out of Brockway onto the open range, their search began to feel like a hopeless task. Ahead of them stretched the endless prairie as far as they could see. The grassland seemed to swallow the pickup truck as it bounced and shook its way down a dirt track.

They followed the track until it ended and then drove alongside animal trails as they inched their way up coulees and around large hills. The farther they went, the more somber Clarice's face became as she leaned out the window, scanning the land.

"Duke!" she hollered. "Duke! Here boy!" She would go silent for moment and then she would call for her horse again.

"We have to find him," Clarice said. "Who knows where Duke could be headed? And if he makes his way to a ranch, who knows what could happen to him then?"

An hour and a half later Clarice thought she saw something up ahead. "Dad, stop the truck," she said. She jumped out of the cab and shielded her eyes from the sun with her hands. It was at least a mile away, but she saw something moving, a small dot on the hillside.

As the pickup moved closer to the hillside, they saw

Duke grazing in the grass near a stand of cottonwoods. Clarice jumped out of the pickup and ran to her horse, reaching up to give him a hug.

"Bad boy," she lectured. There was a smile on her lips. "Don't ever do that again, I could have lost you for good."

The Andersons soon discovered Duke's ingenious method for escape. He would choose a vulnerable fence post, and then he would begin rubbing his side against the post, loosening its footing in the ground. When the post was tilted enough toward the ground, Duke would step back and look at the lowered wire. Then he would circle the pasture in a fast trot before breaking into a gallop, charging directly at the lowered fence and easily jumping over it. Once on the outside, Duke would momentarily stop and glance at the pasture, perhaps waiting for Clarice to appear. And when Clarice didn't show up, Duke would shake his head sideways and gallop off onto the prairie.

Justin saw the entire routine one morning as he prepared to go to work. He roused Clarice from her sleep and they jumped in the pickup, following Duke onto the range once again.

As school began, Duke's escape escapades continued. Each time he jumped out of his pasture, Clarice and Eric would get in the pickup with their father and head out after him. To Eric, the searches began to feel like a giant game of hide and seek on the prairie.

Then one day came a call from the company that owned the elevator where Justin worked. The company wanted him to manage another elevator in North Dakota.

The Andersons were moving again. In the days that followed, as the Andersons started packing, Clarice became strangely quiet. Finally she told her parents they should try to find a new home for Duke in Brockway before they left. After all, Clarice reasoned, the open range was the best place for Duke, and he might not like the more restrictive confines of North Dakota.

"Duke likes to ride on the open range," Clarice said. "Duke hates fences, so he should stay in Montana."

A few days later Clarice sold her stallion to a rancher for $85. Clarice rode Duke out to the rancher's place, but the sale was made final only after the rancher's young daughter climbed up on Duke and rode him around the corral. Clarice knew right then that Duke would be happy on this ranch. She had sold her horse, but even more important than that, Duke had found a new owner, someone he liked.

Clarice hugged her horse goodbye. Her eyes were moist as she climbed into the pickup to leave, but there was also a slight smile on her lips.

She sat in silence for a moment, looking out the window at the stallion. "I feel good about leaving Duke here," she said to her dad. "This will be a good home for him."

As Justin started the pickup to leave, Clarice leaned out her window.

"So long boy!" she shouted to her horse.

Duke pawed the ground and neighed so loud that Clarice's father turned to look as he drove away.

Eric often reminisced the "horse days" in Brockway. And now, as Eric's 13th birthday approached, he thought it was time for him to have his own horse.

It seemed like an appropriate birthday wish now that they lived in Alexander, since the town was surrounded by tall hills and buttes. Looking up from their house, Eric would dream of riding his horse up in the hills one day.

And the thought of riding his horse to the top of Ragged Butte was almost too good to imagine. Eric saw himself and his horse galloping across the top of the butte, dodging boulders and then coming to a sudden halt at the northern edge to look out over the land. It would be just like a scene from a Western movie.

And after the ride on top of the butte we could go down to Jackson Lake. Boy, wouldn't that would be nice? Eric thought.

But as Eric immersed himself in his ongoing dream, a gnawing, doubtful feeling would grow in his stomach. His parents could easily say no to him having a horse. Eric knew little of his family's finances, but he knew they didn't have money to spare. His parents always seemed to buy the cheapest item on the store shelf.

Even Duke was a bargain of sorts. When his parents bought him, they paid only $80. The rancher sold Duke at the discount because of Duke's errant ways.

And when Eric thought back to his previous birthdays, his parents always gave him clothing, a new shirt or pair of pants from JCPenney. If his preceding birthdays were any measure of what was to come, his chances of getting a horse were slim.

Still, he couldn't stop dreaming and he rehearsed his birthday request over and over. Finally, he mustered up the courage to ask. His parents were sitting in the living room, reading the paper, when he approached.

"I'd like to have a horse." He blurted out the words, forgetting his rehearsed request, forgetting to even remind them that his birthday was coming up.

"A what?" his father asked.

"A horse," Eric said. "I'd like to have a horse."

"I don't think so," his father said.

"Why not?"

"We don't have the money for that."

"But lots of kids have horses here," Eric protested. "John has one and Jim has one and so does Dennis. They ride them around town all the time."

"Well, you're not John or Jim or whoever, and our money is tight right now," his father said "We can't buy you one."

Eric's face flushed and his stomach tightened; it felt like someone had punched him in the gut.

"But I really want a horse," Eric protested. His parents sat silently, looking back at him. Eric turned and left the room. He walked out of the house and across the empty lot.

He looked at the half-acre, thinking what a good little pasture it could be. He could build a barbed wire fence around the perimeter. There was a small shack at the far corner where the horse could take shelter from rain, snow and cold weather.

He stopped walking in the middle of the half-acre. The grass was flowing in the wind, almost nonchalantly. Eric's stomach still had that tight feeling as he stepped forward and kicked a rock on the ground.

"Damn it," he muttered, "God damn it!"

He could feel his anger rushing up within him and his eyes were becoming wet. Eric was most angry at his father for the matter-of-fact manner in which he rejected Eric's request for a horse. To Eric, it always seemed as though there was some invisible divide between himself and his father. And it seemed like the divide was growing wider as Eric grew older. Eric scowled at the empty lot.

"You idiot," he said to himself. "You actually thought they would give you a horse."

He suddenly felt foolish for even dreaming of owning a horse. After all, his dad was right; they didn't have extra money. His dad struggled to support his family on his elevator manager's wages. They didn't even own their own house, living instead in the ramshackle homes the elevator company provided.

Before settling in Alexander, the Andersons had been prairie nomads, endlessly moving from one small town to another, always hoping to find something better. But everything always seemed to stay the same.

"Your dad wants to see you," his mother said. She was standing behind Eric and her voice startled him. He turned, wondering how long she had been standing there; he hoped she hadn't heard him curse.

"He wants to talk to you about a horse," she said. Eric's heart seemed to lift a little as he followed his mother back into the house.

"I'll pay you 40 cents an hour to work in the elevator," his father said. "I need someone for the next couple of months to shovel the last of the grain out of the lower bins and also do some other chores around the elevator. If you can save enough money, you can buy your own horse."

There was the slightest smile on his lips. "And I'll talk to Elling Gullickson about letting your horse spend the winter with his livestock on the government pasture."

Eric's mind was racing. *Forty cents an hour times ten hours equals four dollars. If I work fulltime for a week, I could make sixteen dollars!*

"When do you want me to start?" Eric asked.

"Tomorrow after school."

In the weeks that followed, Eric worked after school and on weekends at the elevator. The work was hard and dusty in the bins, almost suffocating at times. He wore goggles and a mask over his nose and mouth as he shoveled grain into a hole in the floor above an auger, then swept the floors bare. He also stacked bags of seed and did other chores. After two and a half months of work at the elevator, Eric figured he had accumulated enough money to buy a good horse. He put a three-line classified advertisement in the McKenzie County Farmer:

> *Wanted: One black horse*
> *Will pay $150*
> *Phone Eric at 692-4338*

Two days later, a rancher called to say he had a horse to sell.

"She's not all black, but she's mostly black, with some white and brown patches," he said. "She's a mare called Moonlight. She's got a crescent-shaped white spot on top of her nose up to her eyes."

A picture of the horse was instantly forming in Eric's mind as he held the phone closer to his ear.

"She's a pretty good horse," the rancher continued. "She doesn't get too spooked about anything."

The telephone line went silent and the rancher cleared his throat as though he were waiting for Eric to speak.

"How much you want for her?" Eric asked.

"One hundred and fifty dollars," the rancher said. "Isn't that what you figured on?"

"Ummmm...you're right," Eric stammered. "When can I get her?"

"My ranch is near Squaw Gap, down in the badlands, but I'll bring her up to your place," the rancher said.

Three days later, Eric came home from school to see Moonlight standing in the driveway beside his parent's car. The horse looked exactly like the rancher described her, mostly black with some patches of brown and white on her sides and back. The crescent-shape white spot stood out prominently above her hose to her eyes.

She seemed very calm standing there as Eric stared at her. There was an old weathered saddle on her back, likely a gift from the rancher, and she wore a bridle, with the reins fastened to the door handle of the car.

Eric surveyed every part of his horse. Her back was slightly sloped, her body was slender and her legs looked strong. Her long tail swayed behind her. He walked to the horse and stroked her head, moving his hand over the white crescent and then scratching under her chin. Her eyes were focused on Eric, and they stared silently at each other for a moment.

"You're a beauty, Moonlight," he said. "Boy, are we going to have fun."

In the weeks that followed, Eric rode Moonlight every day when he got home from school. On weekends they disappeared into the surrounding hills, returning home only as the sun began to set. At times when they were riding, Eric would pull Moonlight to a stop; then he would pinch himself in the arm.

"Yup, it's real," he'd say laughing. Eric was a happy boy and he was quickly bonding with his horse.

Their favorite ride was to the farm of Eric's friend, Jim Gunderson, which was only a mile from town. The Gunderson farm sat at the bottom of a low valley. Tub Butte rose up to the southeast of the farm and Ragged Butte was only a half-mile to the north. It was perfect terrain for two boys on their horses.

Moonlight had an added reason for enjoying riding out to the Gunderson farm. She especially liked Jim's stallion, Dandy.

It was the first hot day of May when Eric and Moonlight galloped down the road for another outing from the Gunderson place. The sky was bright blue, with some scattered cumulous clouds to the east. Eric slowed Moonlight to a trot as they rode up to the house.

The screen door swung open and Jim ran out of the house, wiping his mouth with his hand, looking like he had just finished breakfast.

"I guess you wanna go riding?" Jim asked.

"Yep," Eric said, grinning. "And shake a leg. Moonlight is anxious to see Dandy."

Jim grinned and opened the corral gate. He led Dandy out and handed the reins up to Eric who still sat on his horse. "Here, hold onto him until I get the saddle."

Jim emerged from the corral again, this time holding a saddle half as big as he was. Jim's saddle was beautiful, shiny black leather with silver buttons embedded in lines, forming a border around the top. He grunted loudly as he tossed it onto Dandy's back and in a few minutes they rode out of the farm. They followed a trail to the north through the low valley leading to Ragged Butte.

"Eeeehaaaaa!" Jim suddenly shouted as he and Dandy broke into a gallop.

Moonlight lunged forward into a gallop, following them, not waiting for Eric's command. She was running full speed right behind Dandy.

Eric was pulling hard on the reins, trying to regain control of Moonlight. After several hard tugs Moonlight finally began to slow and they dropped back farther behind Dandy.

They continued to gallop down the trail, but Eric felt much better now. He was in control now and the tense feeling in his arms vanished as they rode up to the base of Ragged Butte. They stopped alongside Jim and Dandy and looked up the eastern slope.

"Let's follow that coulee over there," Jim said, pointing to his right.

Their horses slowly started moving up the steep slope, Jim and Eric leaning forward in their saddles as they climbed. Moonlight seemed sure footed as she casually stepped through the broken rock and around the gopher and badger holes. She'd likely crossed terrain like this many times in the badlands.

They reached the top of Ragged Butte and began exploring the rocky nooks and crannies and circling around the larger boulders. Finally, the boys dismounted on the northern edge of the summit and let their horses graze on the thinning grass. It was just as Eric had dreamed it would be.

The boys sat on a flat rock, looking northward. The prairie had a green tinge to it and the sky was turning a pale blue as the sun rose higher. The cumulous clouds had moved to the south and were forming into thunderheads.

"How do you like your horse?" Jim asked.

"She's good," Eric said. "I'm still getting to know her. But one thing I know for sure, she sure likes Dandy."

Jim grinned and they looked at their horses grazing nearby. Moonlight's head was only inches from Dandy's head as they pulled at the grass.

"This is really neat," Eric said, relaxing on the rock, looking out over the plains below. "I've dreamed of riding a horse up here for a long, long time."

Jim shrugged and stood. "I'm hot," he said. "What say we ride down to Jackson Lake and go for a swim?"

They mounted their horses and moved slowly down the slope, this time sliding backwards in their saddles. When they reached the valley floor, Jim and Dandy broke into a gallop again and headed toward the lake.

"Yeeeeehaaaa Dandy!" Jim shouted. "We're going swimming."

Eric and Moonlight galloped after them through the shrub brush and small trees that led to the lake. Eric liked to ride Moonlight in a gallop; her hooves pounding the ground with a certain rhythm, a fast and graceful forward motion. He sat relaxed on her back, his body moving in unison with his horse as they rode down the trail.

When they reached the lake, they stopped at a grassy clearing between some trees. Jim slid down from his horse and began taking his clothes off; Jim was never one to linger. Eric also jumped down, dropping Moonlight's reins. She began to move to where Dandy was grazing.

Eric took off his clothes and dived into the water after Jim. The water was bracing.

"Whoa," Eric shouted. "This water's cold!"

The boys swam farther out in the lake and turned onto their backs, floating idly and staring up at the sky. Gradually the water began to feel less cold once they got used to it.

Suddenly they heard a loud splashing sound. They turned to see Dandy swimming toward them.

"Dandy!" Jim shouted. "Get out of the water! The saddle!" Jim swam to his horse, grabbed the reins and began pulling his horse back toward shore. Once they moved onto the bank, Jim removed the saddle and sat it on a large rock, then wiped it dry with his T-shirt.

"Damn it Dandy," he said. "You're going to get me in trouble."

Jim looked worried as he turned to Eric. "My dad's going to be real mad if he finds out I let Dandy go in the water with the saddle. He bought me the saddle for Christmas, and my mom said it cost a bundle."

Jim shook his head. "Don't say nothin' about it, okay?"

Eric nodded and looked at the weathered gray saddle still on Moonlight's back. The saddle looked old and decrepit, especially as Moonlight stood grazing next to the rock where Jim's black saddle lay glistening in the sun. Eric swam to the shore and went to Moonlight, removing the saddle. Then he took the bridle off her head.

"Come on girl," Eric said, motioning her with his hand as he waded back into the water. "Let's go for a swim."

Moonlight started to follow him then stopped at the edge of the water. Eric suddenly noticed how beautiful she looked standing there without the worn old saddle on her back. Moonlight lowered her head to smell the water, the wind ruffling her mane and her tail swaying gracefully. She looked like she was debating whether to go in the water.

Moonlight stepped cautiously forward then plunged into the water, swimming out to where Eric was. Her nose brushed his shoulder as she swam past him.

"That a girl," Eric hollered as he swam after her.

Moonlight stopped in the middle the lake where there was a submerged sandbar. She stood resting on the sandbar, the water coming up almost to her back. Eric swam to her neck, grabbed hold and swung up over her back. At first it felt strange to be sitting naked on his horse in the middle of Jackson Lake.

"This is probably how the Indians went swimming with their ponies," he shouted to Jim who was leading Dandy back into the water without the saddle.

There was a loud splash as Dandy plunged back in, followed by Jim. They swam out to the sandbar where Eric sat on top of Moonlight.

The boys and their horses spent a lazy afternoon swimming in Jackson Lake. The boys took turns climbing up on their horses' backs and diving into the water, seeing who could dive the farthest. Then Eric and Jim swam to the far end of the lake and explored the shoreline, searching for water snakes and frogs. A while later the boys swam to the sandbar where the horses still stood.

Suddenly Dandy's tail was raised straight up as he defecated into the water.

"Horse shit!" Jim hollered. "I'm outta here!"

Jim and Eric quickly swam away from their horses and to shore. As they emerged from the water they both stood laughing, slapping their sides.

"Holy crap," Jim said. "I'm glad I wasn't swimming near Dandy's ass when he did that."

Eric wrinkled his nose at the thought "You need to

teach your horse some manners," he said. "No shitting in the lake."

They were laughing so hard they began rolling on the grass, holding their sides.

"Dandy," Jim said in a mocking, solemn voice. "There's absolutely no shitting allowed in this lake. You should know that."

They continued rolling on the grass in laughter. Finally Eric stood, still chuckling, and looked out on the water. Dandy and Moonlight began swimming around the lake in a wide circle.

Eventually Dandy and Moonlight swam to the grassy clearing and walked out of the lake, water dripping from their sides. Jim had walked into the nearby bushes to take a piss and Eric sat alone, watching the horses.

The air above the lake was growing warmer, the sky a pale blue. Moonlight nuzzled Dandy as they stood eating grass, their tails flowing in the breeze. The only sounds were meadowlarks calling to one another in the bushes above the lake.

At that moment, it seemed to Eric that everything was exactly right in the world.

This is nice, he thought. *No, this is better than nice. This is sweet as hell.*

The ride to Ragged Butte and Jackson Lake was one of many adventures for Eric and Moonlight that summer. They spent the long, warm days riding everywhere.

On hot days, Eric would saddle up Moonlight and ride the short distance to Lonesome Lagoon. He would leave

Moonlight to graze on the banks of Lonesome Creek, immediately downstream from the lagoon.

Lonesome Lagoon was too small for a group of boys and a horse, and if Moonlight defecated or urinated in the water, Eric knew he would be very unpopular with the Lonesome Lagoon gang. None of this seemed to matter to Moonlight who would stand quietly eating the thick grass alongside the creek.

On other days Eric and Moonlight rode to Gunderson's farm, meeting up with Jim and Dandy for more excursions to Ragged Butte and the surrounding countryside.

It was the best summer Eric had ever had, and as it neared an end, Eric began to dread sending Moonlight to the government pasture for the winter. Still, his father kept reminding him that winter was coming and Eric needed to take Moonlight out to Elling Gullickson's ranch so she could go with Elling's livestock out on the pasture.

"I've talked to Elling and he says Moonlight can come out," his father said. "So all you have to do is ride Moonlight out to Elling's place. Then call me and I'll drive out and pick you up."

"But why can't I keep Moonlight in town during winter?" Eric asked. "I can fix up the shelter for her in the corner of her pasture and we can buy some hay to feed her through the winter."

"She'll be better off on the government pasture," his dad said. "There's lots of grass there, even in winter, so she'll have plenty to eat. And when winter storms come, she'll take shelter with the other livestock in the trees and bushes in the coulees. Plus there will be other horses there to keep Moonlight company."

Eric was surprised and impressed by what his father said. His father had obviously thought about this matter and it sounded like he knew what he was talking about. After all, he had grown up on a farm himself, and his family had several horses.

"Believe me, it will be much better for Moonlight to spend the winter out there than here in town," his father said. "She'll be much more comfortable out there."

Two weeks latter Eric saddled up Moonlight and they rode out of Alexander on the gravel road leading to the Gullickson ranch. As they followed the road, the land seemed to empty out, the distances growing longer between the scattered farms and ranches. Eric looked over the rolling hills, but there were no landmarks, only grassland and an occasional field where wheat or barley had recently been harvested.

The land reminded Eric of eastern Montana; it was big, open and empty of people. Duke would have liked it here, and Eric wondered if Clarice had ever thought about that.

An hour and half later, they rode into the ranch. Elling Gullickson walked out of the house to greet them. "How ya doing?" he asked. Elling's voice was softer than most ranchers, a strange mixture of a Western drawl sprinkled with a Norwegian accent.

"I'm pretty good," Eric said. "We didn't see much on our way out, just a couple cows is all."

"You betcha," Elling agreed. "I already moved most

of the cattle to the government pasture, plus I got three horses out there."

"I'll drive my pickup out to the pasture," Elling continued. "You can follow me and then we'll let Moonlight get acquainted with the other horses before we leave her there."

Eric followed Elling's pickup back out of the ranch to the gravel road, where he turned south. As they rode down the road, the land became all grassland; there were no cultivated fields in sight. The hills stood brown and the trees in the coulees and alongside the creek beds were bare.

Soon they approached a cattle guard crossing the roadway. It was the entrance to the government pasture, and there was a small gate to the side of the cattle guard where livestock could enter. The land was original prairie, preserved by the government, which allowed area ranchers to run their livestock on the land for a fee.

Elling drove his pickup off the road onto a small dirt trail that led up the side of a hill. When he reached the top he stopped and got out of the pickup. Eric and Moonlight rode up and watched Elling, who was surveying the land below. The rancher brought his fingers to his mouth and made a shrill whistle, which seemed to echo down the hillside. Then he reached inside the pickup and honked the horn several times.

"They'll come in a minute," Elling said. "They're probably down in a draw somewhere horsing around." He snickered out loud at his own joke before raising his fingers to his mouth again to whistle.

Fifteen minutes later three horses suddenly appeared on a nearby hillside. Moonlight turned to look at them and Eric began removing her saddle and bridle. She stood motionless at his side, staring at the horses.

"Go ahead, girl," Eric said. "Go meet them. Those are your new friends."

He gave Moonlight a little swat on her back and she ran off to the other horses. As she approached them the horses seemed to form a group around her and they began sniffing and circling each other.

"Come on, get in," Elling told Eric as he got into his pickup. They drove across the hill to a spot closer to the horses. Then Elling got out of the pickup and grabbed a pail. He opened a sack of oats in the truck bed and poured it into the pail.

"This is like an ice cream treat to a horse," he said, grinning. "I always give them some oats for coming to me when I call them. It's like payola."

Elling chuckled as he walked to the horses, allowing each to eat some oats from the pail. Then he gave some to Moonlight. Eric kept looking at Moonlight; she seemed at home here. Maybe the open grassland reminded her of her previous home in the badlands.

Still, Eric was worried about how his horse would fare out here in the long, cold winter. He tried to look unconcerned about all these things as he walked to Moonlight and began stroking her head.

"Well, it's time we go," Elling said. "I gotta get back to the ranch and do some things."

Eric's stomach tightened a little, but he continued stroking Moonlight's head for a few moments. He didn't want to leave. Moonlight was looking straight at him, just like the first time they saw each other.

"I'll come back and see you soon, girl," Eric said. "Have fun with your new friends."

He turned to walk to pickup, half expecting Moonlight to follow him. But she stood with the other horses on the hillside, still staring at him. Then she whinnied and turned to begin sniffing the other horses once again.

"You can come out and ride her whenever you want," Elling said as Eric climbed into the cab. If I'm not home you know where the oats are so just help yourself. And I'll leave your saddle and bridle hanging in the feed room."

Eric nodded as Elling started the pickup, which lurched forward as they began bouncing down the hill.

"How's that saddle working out?" Elling asked. "I know it ain't much, but it's the only spare one I had."

Eric's eyes widened as he looked at Elling. "It works fine," he said. "I didn't know you gave the saddle to me. Thanks a lot."

"You betcha," Elling said. "But don't thank me too much, that saddle is beat all to hell and not worth much. But at least you can use it till your dad gets you something better."

"You betcha," Eric said, grinning back at Elling.

Eric wondered why his dad hadn't told him that Elling gave him the saddle; and he was certain his dad would never buy him a new one.

Eric turned for one last look at Moonlight, but she and the other horses were gone. The hill stood empty with only the prairie grass flowing in the wind.

———— ————

Eric returned to the government pasture several times that winter to see his horse. Clarice, who now had her driver's license, would drive him to ranch where Eric retrieved the saddle, bridle and a pail of oats.

Then they we would drive into the government pasture and park on the hill where they last saw Moonlight. Clarice would honk the horn several times, while Eric waited outside the car. Sure enough, Moonlight always showed up. Moonlight looked content and she was also happy to eat the oats as Eric put the saddle on her back. Then they would go for a ride. Eric noticed that Moonlight seemed to have a lot of energy and she liked to gallop at a very fast pace. It appeared that his dad was right; this was the best place for Moonlight to spend the winter.

In early April, Eric told his father he thought it was time to bring Moonlight back to town for the summer. His father suggested he wait one more month, but when he saw the disappointed look on Eric's face, he agreed they could go get Moonlight.

As they drove into the Gullickson ranch, Eric saw Moonlight standing in the corral.

Elling was in a shed next to the corral, and he came out to greet them as they drove up.

"I brought all my livestock in off the government pasture last week," Elling said. "There's not much grass left out there."

Eric's father nodded and then he and Elling went into the house for coffee. Eric, who was anxious to bring Moonlight back to town for another summer, was already saddling up Moonlight

The summer began much like the previous one ended. Eric would often ride Moonlight out to Jim's place, Jim would saddle up Dandy, and they'd head out for another ride on the plains. As the summer progressed, they explored greater distances until they reached Timber Creek, which meandered through a wide low valley heading north to the Missouri River.

Eric saddled up Moonlight one warm morning to ride out to Jim's place again. The weather forecast called for a hot day, so Eric planned to meet up with Jim and ride to Lonesome Lagoon to swim.

"Hey, Eric, going swimming?"

Eric turned to see Lynn Fjelstad standing behind him. Lynn's red mongrel dog stood by his side.

"I think so," Eric answered. "But first, Moonlight and me are riding out to the Gundersons to join up with Jim and Dandy."

Eric waved to Lynn and turned, tapping his legs against Moonlight's side. Then he saw something move below and he heard a sudden growl, followed by a shrill scream from Moonlight. She kicked her rear legs and then there were more growling noises below.

Suddenly, Moonlight began to buck, leaping off the ground and arching her back upward. Eric tightened his legs and pulled on the reins.

There was more growling and Moonlight bucked again. Eric clung to the saddle horn and tightened the reins, trying to control Moonlight, but she arched her back and bucked even higher.

Moonlight's shrill screams filled the air as everything suddenly seemed to be spinning out of control.

Her feet landed on the ground with another loud thud, and then she bucked upward again. Eric heard a loud snapping noise, and it seemed like he was rising even higher. He glanced down to see Moonlight below him as he flew away from her.

Moonlight had bucked so hard that the cinch securing the saddle had broken. In an instant, Eric and the saddle were plunging back to earth. He stretched his arms out, trying to brace himself as he slammed into the ground.

Eric's body slid forward from the impact and rolled to a stop. He lay still until he felt the pain rise up from his shoulder and his body tensed.

"Uhhhhhhh," he moaned. He was gasping for air, but he couldn't breathe. He finally drew a short breath and heard Lynn shouting something above him. Eric lifted his head to see Moonlight.

She was running fast toward the fence on the far side of the pasture, the mongrel still at her heels. Eric watched in horror as Moonlight ran straight into the barbed wire. There was a blurring motion as her legs flew out from under her and she flipped over the wire in a grotesque cartwheel.

Her large body slammed into the ground in a cloud of dust. Moonlight lay motionless, wrapped in twisted wire and uprooted fence posts. The mongrel was retreating as a rock struck him in the side, thrown by Lynn.

"Moonlight!" Eric screamed. He pulled himself up to a half crouching position; he felt a sharp pain in his shoulder and couldn't move his right arm, but he began stumbling toward her.

"Moonlight!" he screamed again.

There was throbbing pain in Eric's shoulder and blood was dripping from his forehead. He knew he was hurt badly, but at that moment the only thing that mattered to Eric was his horse.

As he drew closer he could see Moonlight was still on the ground, wrapped in the barbed wire. Pools of blood were forming around her.

"Where's that stupid mutt?" Eric screamed as he turned. The dog was already at the far fence, fleeing from more rocks. "I'll kill you, you dirty piece of crap!"

Eric blinked as he wiped blood from his eyebrows with his left hand. He turned toward Moonlight; she was still struggling, wrapped in the tangled wire. She looked like she was trying to stand. As he approached, Eric heard her whinny, a soft, helpless sound.

"Moonlight," he called as he staggered forward. "I'm

coming. Don't move."

As Eric came closer, he could see the deep cuts on Moonlight's side. Blood was smeared on her side and covered part of the crescent on her nose. Eric began to sob.

"Moonlight," he whispered as he dropped to his knees beside her. Tears were flowing down his cheeks, mixing with the blood and dirt on his face and dripping onto his hands.

"Moonlight," he whispered again. She raised her head to face him, her eyes wide with shock, and then she laid her head back on the ground. Eric saw her side was quivering in pain.

"I'm going to get you out of this mess," he said. "You're going be okay."

Eric reached for a strand of wire, but then his world suddenly went dark.

"Are you waking up?"

"Eric, open your eyes so I can see you."

The words echoed in a dark space, but Eric rolled his head slightly to the side, trying to face the voice.

"Come on Eric, open your eyes and talk to me."

Eric struggled, trying to respond. He felt his eyelids open, but all he saw were shades of gray. He opened his mouth and tried to speak, but nothing came out. The shades of gray turned black, but he could still hear the voices.

"Can you see me?" someone asked.

Small yellow strands of light suddenly appeared, moving across the black and gray mass. A dull image was slowly forming. It looked like something above him.

"I'm going to shine this light in your eyes for a minute." It was the voice of a man and it smelled of coffee.

Eric's sight grew clearer and now he could see a man bent over him. It looked like he was putting a small flashlight back in his shirt pocket.

"You're doing good, cowboy," he said. There was some laughter in the background. "You're going to be back at the saddle before you know it." There was more laughter.

Eric could see the man's eyes were blue and intense, his dark hair hung down on his forehead as he bent over Eric.

"I'm Dr. Wold," he said. "You've been out for a while."

The doctor put his hand on Eric's forehead and left it there as though he was trying to find something. Then he looked closely at Eric's eyes, almost as though he was trying to see inside Eric's head.

Eric heard feet shuffling and saw his parents at the doctor's side. His father's face was somber and his mother looked worn, like she hadn't slept. She smiled weakly as they stepped closer.

"How you doing?" his mother asked, touching his arm.

"I'm okay, Ma," Eric muttered. As Eric spoke he noticed a thick mass of tape wrapped over his shoulder.

"You broke your collar bone," Dr. Wold explained. "It'll be sore as the devil for a few days, but then it'll start to get better."

The doctor stepped forward and grabbed Eric's wrist to feel his pulse. "You also have a concussion from bouncing your head on the ground," the doctor said.

Eric grinned at the doctor, but then his memory suddenly came racing back and the grin vanished from Eric's face.

The growling mongrel, the loud snapping noise, the ground rushing up, the painful thud on the ground. The blood, the dirt, the tears...

And Moonlight...

She was on the ground, tangled in a horrific mass of wire, struggling to free herself.

Eric's body began to shake. He tried to speak, but there was no air. He turned to his parents as the terrible memories kept flooding back. He could think only of Moonlight lying helplessly on the ground, her eyes wide with fear.

"And what happened next?" he asked, staring at his parents. "How is Moonlight?"

Both his parents moved closer, looking down at Eric.

"Is Moonlight okay?" Eric shouted the words at them, the pitch so loud it sent a sharp pain across his chest.

"She broke her leg when she hit the fence," his father

said. "Moonlight is gone."

"What?" Eric screamed. "What do you mean she's gone? I saw her on the ground. She was trying to get up. She just needed to get untangled!"

"She's gone," his father repeated. "I had to put her down. I'm sorry, Eric."

"You shot Moonlight?" Eric's face instantly turned to hate. "No! You couldn't have. No!"

More pain flashed across Eric's chest as he continued to shout at his parents. His body tightened as he struggled to get out of the bed, but the doctor stepped forward, placing both hands on Eric's chest and forcing him back down on the bed.

"Whoa there," the doctor scolded. "You've got to settle down. You *must* calm down." The doctor's face was only inches from Eric's face as he spoke. A needle pricked Eric's arm and he turned to see the nurse firmly holding his arm flat on the bed while the fluid emptied into his arm.

Eric ignored the doctor, turning to face his parents.

"Why did you do it?" the words seemed to echo across the room as Eric spoke. Suddenly his voice was losing its strength and he was becoming woozy.

He could feel the tension easing in his body as the effects of the drug began to take hold. He slumped flat on the bed, his anger suddenly gone. His body was becoming limp, and he welcomed the coming darkness, the dull nothingness that approached. It would be a welcome break from this nightmare.

And the wrenching pain would still be there when he awakened.

———

After three days in the hospital, Dr. Wold told Eric he could go home.

"The effects of your concussion are almost gone," he said. "You are less disorientated, you've been sleeping less and your memory is obviously back. I want you to leave your right arm in the sling for two weeks until your collar bone heals."

He smiled a little as he looked at Eric's bruised face. "All those scabs on your face will soon fall off and you'll be as good-looking as ever. Just remember to stay in the saddle next time, and you won't be bouncing your head on the ground."

The doctor chuckled and turned to Eric's mother. "Bring him back in three days and I'll remove the bandages and check him out again."

Eric slid out of bed and his mother helped him put on his clothes. The window on the side of the room was being pelted by raindrops.

"It's really coming down this morning," his mother said. She was smiling slightly, but Eric's face was grim.

"Did she suffer?" he asked.

The question caught his mother by surprise, but she maintained her calm. She seemed to be searching for the right words as she slid Eric's shirt over his bandaged shoulder.

"Moonlight went very quickly," she said. "Her misery was ended and you should know it was hard for your dad to put her down, but he had no choice. And I'll never forget the look on your dad's face after he did it."

Eric's mother had found a way to scold him, and he knew he deserved it.

"I'm sorry," Eric said as he stood. He walked into the bathroom, pausing in front of the mirror, examining his bruised face. Large scabs covered much of his forehead and the left side of his jaw. His right arm rested in a large white sling hanging from his neck and shoulders. His eyes looked hollow and blank.

God, you're ugly, a real mess, he thought.

As he lingered there, examining himself in the mirror, he thought he could almost forgive Dr. Wold for making all his cowboy jokes.

Eric and his mother walked out of the room and down the hallway. They were greeted by nurses and aides as they walked by them. Several staff members stepped forward to pat Eric gently on his free arm, and one nurse temporarily blocked his path and planted a sudden kiss on Eric's bruised jaw.

"You go get 'em cowboy," someone shouted. "Happy trails."

Eric smiled slightly, looking straight ahead, and he waved goodbye to them over his shoulder without looking back. He and his mother walked out of the hospital and ran through the rain to the car.

As Eric slid into the seat, he recalled Dr. Wold's advice. "Just remember to stay in saddle next time and you won't be bouncing your head on the ground."

Little did the doctor know how untrue and hollow his joke was; Moonlight didn't buck Eric out of the saddle, it was the cinch of the saddle that broke, launching both Eric and the saddle skyward. And as Eric sat in the car, he wondered what might have happened had the cinch held and had he managed to stay on top Moonlight.

Maybe I could have controlled her bucking while Lynn chased his dog away. I could have calmed Moonlight. I would have dismounted and stroked her mane and said soothing words to her.

Eric's mind was racing as he considered all sorts of scenarios. It seemed like he was searching for a piece to a puzzle. Then he remembered his conversation with Elling the day he had thanked the rancher for giving him the saddle.

"You betcha," Elling said. "But don't thank me too much, that saddle is beat all to hell and not worth much. But at least you can use it 'til your dad gets you something better."

Eric nodded his head in silence. He'd found the missing piece. His face turned dark and brooding as he looked through the car window at the falling rain. He felt his body tighten as his anguish and anger came rushing back.

Chapter 5

Bestefar

"I picked Hannah up at the train depot in Ray, and we climbed into my wagon for the long ride out to the farm. The day was cool and windy, and Hannah pulled a hat from her bag to shield her eyes from the bright sun.

"Hannah seemed uneasy as she looked out over the prairie. 'Nils, are there any Indians here?' she asked.

"I told her I had seen only a few small bands passing by as they moved to the Fort Berthold Reservation.

"When we arrived at the homestead I showed her our temporary house, a large dugout in the ground. Lodge poles held a sod roof over the top of the dugout. I lifted the trap door on the roof and we climbed down the ladder; it was cool, damp and somewhat dark inside. When Hannah reached the bottom, she stepped off the ladder and turned to look at the place. I told her the coolness in the dugout would be nice on a hot day. When I saw the disappointed look on Hannah's face, I assured her the dugout was only our temporary home until I could build us a wooden house.

"That seemed to make her feel a little better, but when we went to bed that night she became frightened when the prairie wolves began to howl, which they often did at night. Then a clump of sod fell down from the ceiling of the dugout, landing flat on Hannah's leg, Startled, she jumped out of the bed, lit the lantern and examined the fallen sod.

"Then suddenly her body shook and she began to cry. I hugged her, trying to comfort her, but she continued to cry for a long, long time."

———— ————

Eric's grandfather was a big man, with a Viking physique. More than 6 feet tall, with broad shoulders and arms still as thick as gate posts, he walked with a slow but determined pace. His salt-and-pepper hair was surprisingly curly, especially for a Norwegian.

Bestefar was the father of Eric's mother. His christened name was Nils Berge, but everyone in Inga's family called him "Bestefar," which is "best of fathers" in Norwegian. Some traditions disappear slowly in Norwegian-American culture, and the name Bestefar was still used by Eric's family two generations after he immigrated to America.

Even in his old age, Bestefar still had a sure and sturdy look about him. In his pocket he carried a good luck charm, the lead from a bullet he fired to kill a bear that charged him on a mountain trail in Norway.

As a young man he was very athletic and known as a strong swimmer. While he was working as a fisherman, saving his money so he could come to America, another man was washed off his boat in stormy seas near the Lofoten Islands. Bestefar dove into the icy sea and swam through giant waves to pull the man back to safety. It seemed as though Bestefar was indestructible. He really was the best of everything.

On the day of Bestefar's 90th birthday, Eric's family drove from Alexander to his farm in Rainbow Valley to celebrate with him. Bestefar still lived on the farm 15 years after his wife, Hannah, died. He shared the house with his bachelor son, Jonas, who also ran the farm.

The Andersons' car bounced and shook as it moved down the rough gravel road. It was spring, and the newly seeded crops were coming up in the fields, forming a bright green mantle with a fresh, new scent that permeated the plains.

"Now, when we get there, remember not to get in Bestefar's way," Eric's mother, Inga, said. "He needs a clear path; he can't walk as well as he used to."

Eric's father, Justin, turned the car off the county road and through a narrow stand of cottonwoods. The farmhouse sat in the middle of a clearing, with a barn and shed off to one side. A shelterbelt, rows of trees and shrubs, surrounded the farm, providing a break from the prairie wind and also catching and holding drifting winter snow.

The farmhouse, with two floors, was a sturdy structure. A chimney anchored the rear of the house, and a large porch wrapped around the front. Bestefar built the house himself many years ago after homesteading on this land. Behind the barn lay the wooden wheels from his original wagon, which his horses first pulled across the prairie to this very spot.

Bestefar stood smiling on the porch as the Andersons pulled up to the house and got out of their car.

"God dag, Justin and Inga," Bestefar said, nodding to Eric's parents.

"God dag," their father said. " Hvordan har De det?"

"I'm fine," Bestefar answered in English.

Bestefar bent slightly to greet Eric, Clarice and Caroline, and then they all went into the house.

Their parents, Bestefar and Jonas stood in the parlor, conversing in their usual mix of English and Norwegian. They seemed more comfortable speaking Norwegian. There was another factor involved, too: In Eric's family, his parents spoke Norwegian when they didn't want the children to know what they were saying.

"Let's go check the roast," Inga said to Jonas, who had started cooking the roast earlier. As Inga and Jonas went into the kitchen, Justin also left the room to smoke a cigarette on the porch. Eric and his sisters suddenly stood alone with Bestefar in the parlor.

"How long until dinner?" Bestefar shouted toward the kitchen.

"About an hour," their mother hollered back.

He motioned to Eric, Clarice and Caroline to move closer. "Come sit down," he said. "I'll tell you a story before dinner; a story from the old days." He sat in his leather chair in the corner, leaning his cane on the arm. Eric and his sisters sat on the sofa facing him.

Norwegians love to tell stories, and Bestefar, true to his name, was the best story teller Eric and his sisters had ever known.

The old man seemed to be gathering his thoughts as

he sat in silence for a moment. Then he began.

"When Hannah and I first came to North Dakota, the law had not yet come to this land," he said. "People could do as they pleased.

"Almost all of the homesteaders were law-abiding and came here only to farm the land. But there were also a few thieves who roamed the land, looking for things to steal. And then there were the rough and tumble cowboys who liked to drink and fight. Sometimes, if a cowboy lost all his cash in a poker game or spent all his money on liquor, he too would resort to thievery.

"So whenever I would go away from our farm, leaving Hannah at home with the children, she would fret ever so much. One of the first things she did when I left was she would hang blankets over the windows so no one could see inside our house.

"Hannah was especially afraid of the cowboys when they passed by, driving herds of cattle to the stockyard at the railroad in Ray. The cowboys wore leather chaps and wide-brimmed hats and cursed an awful lot. Hannah had never seen anything like them in Norway. Sometimes when the cowboys passed by, they would stop and ask for food. Although Hannah regarded these men as vulgar and loud, she always agreed to give them something to eat.

"Still, Hannah never allowed the cowboys in her house, instructing them to wait at the front door. Then she would go inside and prepare beef sandwiches and rolls of buttered lefse.

"Returning to the doorway, she would hand the food

to the cowboys and send them on their way. Bestefar paused for a moment and chuckled softly. "Unknown to the cowboys, Hannah also had a loaded 16-guage shotgun leaning against the wall inside the kitchen door. And she knew how to use it.

"Although it was the cowboys that scared Hannah the most, there were also other strangers passing by our farm," he continued. "Young men would walk from farm to farm, asking for work. Most of these men were good, honest souls, they were only seeking work, but some of them had other things in mind. Some were simply thieves in disguise, waiting for the right moment to steal things from a farmer, sometimes even making off with the farmer's cows in the middle of the night."

Bestefar paused and his face suddenly seemed to harden. "And occasionally these men who wandered across the plains did very bad things."

Nils and Hannah Berge's nearest neighbors were Otto and Mabel Sanderson and their daughter, Lilly. The Sanderson farm was only a half-mile south of the Berge farm, and the two families became close friends since the parents had all emigrated from Norway in the 1890s and early 1900s. The two families had much in common as they began a new life on their homestead land in North Dakota.

When the Sandersons first staked their homestead claim, they built a sod house. The house was made of large cubes of top soil, cut from the ground and stacked like bricks for walls. The roof was framed with lodge poles and covered with more sod.

The Sandersons lived in their small sod house for three long years, saving their profits from their grain harvest each fall. Finally they had saved enough money to buy the timber for their house and hire some carpenters to help Otto build it.

In 1903, Otto and the carpenters built a fine wood-frame house. The house went up rather quickly, and Otto and the carpenters then built a small barn nearby for the milk cows. When construction was completed and the carpenters' wages paid, the Sandersons were pleased to see that they still had some money left over. So they decided to purchase 160 acres adjacent to their farm that was owned by Glenn Heggen.

Everything seemed to be going very well for the Sanderson family, but they soon discovered their expanded farm required much more labor. They worked in the fields, plowing the earth and planting seeds from sunup until after dusk. And then they sat exhausted at the super table each night.

So when a tall young stranger stopped at their place one day asking for work, they were immediately interested. The young man said his name was John Singleton.

"You've run a plow behind horses?" asked Mr. Sanderson.

"Sure have, I've done lots of that down in Nebraska," Singleton replied.

"And you've cared for livestock?" Sanderson asked.

"I've done lots of that too," the young man said. "Both cattle and horses and even some oxen along the way."

"Okay, we'll hire you," Sanderson said. "We'll need you at least through the summer and maybe through the fall until the snow flies." Sanderson led Singleton into the house and introduced him to his wife, Mabel, and their 10-year-old daughter, Lilly.

"Welcome to our farm," Mabel said, smiling.

"Thank you," Singleton said. "This will be good for me, working here at your place this summer and maybe through the fall. And when I'm done here I'll probably head back to Nebraska."

The two men shook hands in formal agreement. Mabel began gathering some bedding from a closet, and she and her daughter left the house to fix Singleton a bed in the shack attached to the barn.

That night they all sat down for super, the young man still wearing his worn suit and scuffed shoes. The Sandersons did not think his appearance was unusual, however, since he arrived at their farm on foot, carrying a single bag over his shoulder. He looked like he had been walking for a very long ways.

In the days that followed, the Sandersons were pleased to see that Singleton was a hard worker. He began plowing the new land they acquired from the Heggens. The hired hand worked long days, stopping just in time to wash up before eating the evening meal.

"How did you end up here?" Mr. Sanderson asked at the super table one night. "The Dakotas are a long ways from Nebraska."

Singleton swallowed a mouthful of potatoes, washing it down with his glass of milk.

"I had never been to the Dakotas," he said. "So I thought I'd come up this way and see what's here. The Dakotas look an awful lot like Nebraska."

He smiled and laughed a little before continuing. "It seems like this prairie must run all the way up through Canada," he said, making a sweeping gesture with his hand. "Maybe someday I'll head up there to Canada."

As the summer progressed, supplies began running low at Nils and Hannah's farm. At super one night, Nils told Hannah that he would make the long trip to Ray the following day to buy the feed, seed and other things they needed.

Hannah nodded her agreement, but a frown was already forming on her face. Hannah hated being left home alone with her four young children; the oldest, Jonas, was 10 years old.

To make matters worse, several cattle drives had passed by their farm in recent weeks. Hannah just couldn't shake that uneasy feeling when she saw the cowboys approach, and she still shuddered when she heard them shouting and cursing through the dust clouds at the cattle.

As Nils discussed the individual items they needed, Hannah nodded her concurrence at each item, but a tight, uneasy feeling was growing in her stomach.

They finished eating super and later put the children to bed. Nils went back to the table and continued going over his list of supplies. When he paused to look up he saw the worried look on Hannah's face as she heated their coffee on the stove.

"What's the matter, Hannah? He asked. "What is troubling you?"

"I know we're low on supplies," she replied. "I know you have to go; I just don't feel good about it." Her voice seemed strained as she spoke. She moved a little closer to Nils as he slid his chair back and stood at the table.

"I'm frightened about being home alone with the children," she said.

As Hannah spoke, Nils could see the fear and anguish growing on her face. Suddenly there were tears in her eyes. Nils moved closer and reached out to her, but Hannah stepped back. She was not done speaking.

"It was never like this in Norway," Hannah said. "I never felt in danger in Norway, but here in Dakota anything can happen." The harsh tone was growing in her voice. *"And worst of all, here in Dakota there's no place to hide!"*

Nils went to Hannah and pulled her to him. He held her tightly, caressing her hair and trying to comfort her.

"I know you're frightened," he said softly, "but it will be okay. I'll leave very early in the morning. And when I get to town, I will quickly buy the supplies and hurry home."

Hannah said nothing; she only buried her face in Nils'

chest and cried softly. It seemed there was nothing Nils could say to make her feel better.

When Nils and Hannah went to bed that night they both tossed and turned for hours. Nils dozed on and off, and when he got up the room was still dark. He dressed and went to the barn to harness the horses, hitching them to the wagon. Hannah went downstairs to make breakfast.

When Nils returned to the house they quietly ate their porridge and lefse in the darkened kitchen, which was lit by a single lantern. Then they each drank a large cup of strong coffee. They stared silently at each other across the table before Nils finally rose. He did not like to leave Hannah like this, but it was time for him to go.

They walked to the porch and Nils kissed Hannah goodbye, hugging her tightly. "It's going to be okay," he whispered in her ear. "I'll be back home before you know it."

The sun had yet to rise as Nils drove his team of horses and wagon away from the farm.

Hannah stood on the porch breathing the cool morning air and looking over the prairie. The darkness was beginning to fade with the coming sunrise. When she looked toward the road she could see a faint outline, a silhouette of Nils, his horses and wagon moving.

It was a calm and peaceful sight, she admitted. She felt strangely relaxed at that moment, standing alone in the fading darkness. Dawn was the one time of the day when the prairie winds were still and the land was silent. The silhouette grew smaller as it moved farther down the road.

Hannah wished she could hang onto this moment, but she knew this peaceful feeling would soon end. In a few minutes the sun would begin to rise, casting its bright light into every space. The land would open up and everything on it would be illuminated for everyone to see.

On this day, alone in the middle of this immense prairie, Hannah and her small children would anxiously wait for time to pass. Their eyes would remain fixed on the distant road, looking for the familiar wagon and horses.

She turned to the east. The sky was becoming light and suddenly the sun began to appear, a slice of brightness lifting up from the horizon. As Hannah watched the sunrise, a cold shudder ran down her spine.

Nils arrived in Ray later that morning. He stopped at the livestock tank on the edge of town to water his horses. He had driven his team hard that morning, perhaps too hard, he thought.

He retrieved a brush from the under the wagon seat, dipped it in the tank and began brushing down his horses as they drank.

When the horses appeared rested and watered, he fed then each a pail of oats. Then they drove into town, passing several clapboard homes until they reached Main Street.

Nils moved quickly down the street, first to the feed and seed store and then to the hardware. He crossed items off his list as he bought them and spent little time talking to the merchants.

"Hannah is home alone with the kids, and she's not comfortable with that," Nils explained. "So I'm gathering our supplies as quickly as possible so I can hurry home."

"I don't blame Hannah for being nervous," a woman clerk said at the hardware store. "I would not like to be out there all alone on the prairie. There are too many strangers moving about these days."

She shook her head at this thought. "We see them get off the train here in Ray, some with tattered clothing and worn out shoes," she said. "They look broke and desperate, and I wouldn't want to run into any of them out there on the prairie."

Nils loaded the last of the supplies in the wagon and climbed up in the seat. He tapped the reins slightly on his horses and they began moving down the street. At the very end of the block was the tavern with the covered walkway in front.

As he approached, Nils remembered Hannah's final request. "Please don't stop at the tavern, not even for a single drink," she said. "I want you to come home as soon as possible."

As Nils passed by the tavern, he spotted some friends standing in front on the tavern on the walkway. Nils called out to them as he passed by.

"I've got to get back to the farm," he said. "Hannah is home alone with the kids."

His friends smiled knowingly and waved back. "*Neste tid drinken sitter i du* (next time the drink is on you)," someone hollered.

Nils laughed and waved back. He drove his team to the edge of town then turned north onto the county road. The wagon, heavy with supplies, groaned and made creaking sounds as they continued down the road.

As the day wore on, Nils sat transfixed in his seat staring ahead at the road. He remembered Hannah's frightened face the night before, her tears and her sudden outburst. Her emotions had all poured out at once.

He knew Hannah was having a difficult time adapting to life on the prairie. After all, she came from a prosperous family in Norway. Her father had a dairy farm and they lived in spacious house. The house sat on the side of a hill, overlooking a lake that was surrounded by forest. Hannah had left all that to come to America and ended up settling here on the prairie. Dakota was a land completely different from Norway, and it likely bore no resemblance to her dreams of what America would look like.

Hannah and Nils had met after they immigrated. They had both settled in Starbuck, Minnesota, where Hannah worked as a housemaid and Nils as a carpenter. They were young and fell in love and got married. But when they moved west to homestead in North Dakota, Hannah's dreams of their new life seemed to dull somewhat as she looked at the strange, empty land. Nils, however, saw things differently. He saw 160 acres of fertile land, which was much more than anything he could ever hope to own back in Norway.

Nils had done everything he could to make Hannah comfortable, including building a fine new house.

He knew how much she appreciated it after living in the dugout for nearly a year. Furthermore, their new house was one of the larger homes in Rainbow Valley, providing ample room for their growing family.

Their crops had been good and they had managed to save a little money, putting it in their account at the bank. They even discussed the possibility of some day making a trip back to Norway to visit their families.

In spite of their growing prosperity, Nils knew something still was missing for Hannah. She still longed for the mountains and forests of Norway. But now, when she looked out on this new land, there was only endless prairie from horizon to horizon.

"And there's not a tree in sight," she often said, a bitterness in her voice.

The prairie landscape was so alien to Hannah that she feared the very land itself, almost as much as the cursing cowboys and other strangers who roamed across it.

Nils sensed his wife's uneasiness, but he also believed this would change. Nils was a determined man. Somehow he would help Hannah adapt, and Hannah would soon appreciate this new land, *her new land*. Dakota, with its treeless expanse of grassland, certainly was different from their native Norway, but where else in the world could they have all this? Nils smiled as he looked out at the endless prairie. One day, he thought, Hannah would grow to love the prairie as much as he did.

The wagon continued to creak and groan, raising small clouds of dust. Nils wished he could move his team of horses faster, but the load was too heavy for that.

Nils would never abuse his horses. They were his prize possessions, having brought him to this new land. Almost everything on the farm depended on the horses. They pulled the plows in the fields, hauled supplies to the farm and transported loads of harvested grain to the elevator in town. On Sunday, the horses pulled the wagon with the Berge family to services at the Rainbow Valley Lutheran Church. The horses were everything to the Berge family.

Nils remembered the winter day when his horses pulled the wagon to the coal mine on the bluffs above the Missouri River. The men at the mine filled the wagon with coal, and Nils began the 15-mile trip home. The day was cold and it was snowing. By late afternoon the wind was picking up, raising thick clouds of snow, obstructing his view.

As they trudged on through the gathering storm, Nils was becoming more anxious. He knew they should have arrived at the farm by now, but he could see nothing ahead, only the backs of his horses and clouds of vapor from their breath. Nils continued to drive the team forward through the bitter cold and swirling snow.

Finally, Nils pulled the horses to a stop, admitting he was lost. Even worse, he sensed he was needlessly driving his horses in a wide circle, going nowhere. Nils' body was becoming numb from the cold, the icy snow crystals stinging his face, the air was so frigid it hurt to breath. If he did not find home soon, Nils might freeze to death. He knew the horses would survive. Their thick coats would protect them from the snow and cold. They would wait for the storm to end and when the skies cleared they would walk home, pulling the wagon with Nils' frozen corpse on top.

This gruesome thought gave Nils an idea. He got down from his seat. Then he loosened the reins from the backs of each horse, climbed back into the wagon seat and called down to them.

"Heeehhaaaa," he said. "Let's go home girls. Find the way!"

In less than an hour, Nils' horses, operating on blind instinct and their innate senses, pulled Nils and the wagon filled with coal into the Berge farm.

Nils' horses found the way home after he had failed. They had saved his life, and on that day a bond was formed that would never be broken. Nils now had complete trust in his horses; he grew to love them almost as much as he did Hannah.

And now, on a warm summer day, Nils' beloved horses were serving him once again, pulling a heavy load of supplies back to the farm.

The horses continued moving down the road in their methodical motion. The cloud of dust trailed behind the wagon, lingering as they passed.

Nils was anxious to get home, but he would not drive his team faster because they were pulling a very heavy load. As he sat in his seat, he could only imagine the satisfaction of soon driving his horses and wagon up to the house. The windows would be covered with blankets. Hannah and the children would run out to greet him.

At the Berge farm, Hannah finished eating lunch with the children and put the three youngest down for their naps. Then she and Jonas went out outside to the chicken coop to feed the chickens.

They were spreading seed on the ground in the coop when she heard the first sound, a dull thud that suddenly echoed across the prairie.

Hannah stopped to listen. It sounded like gunfire, but now there was quiet once again, just a few chickens scratching the earth and clucking nearby. Then several more loud thuds rang out; it seemed to be coming from somewhere to the south, but she couldn't be sure. "That's gunfire," Hannah said, dropping her seed to the ground.

"Jonas," she said. "Go to the house, awaken the children and bring them outside."

Jonas stood motionless, his mouth open and a confused look on his face.

"Now!" Hannah shouted at him. Jonas stepped back, opened the chicken coop door and ran for the house.

Hannah latched the door to the coop and began running across the farmyard. She ran to the edge of the shelterbelt and stopped at the root cellar, a dugout in which they stored their vegetables. Hannah reached down and pulled open the door to the cellar.

She turned to see Jonas and the other children running toward her from the house. "Okay," she said as they gathered around. "I want you to go down into the cellar for a little bit. And I want you to wait down there until I say it's okay to come out."

She saw the fear grow on the faces of Peder, Marvel and Inga. They all began to cry.

"Mamma," Marvel cried. "What's wrong?"

Hannah struggled to answer. "I thought I heard something that sounded like gunshots," she said, trying to sound less concerned than she really was. "It's probably something else. But I think you should take cover, just in case there's some crazy cowboy out there shooting his gun in the air."

Her voice trailed off and Hannah knew from the looks on their faces that she had failed to calm them. Their crying was growing louder, and their cheeks were wet with tears.

Hannah felt the maternal instinct to drop to her knees and hug them all, but there was no time for that. She must move quickly to protect them. She swallowed hard, trying to hold back her own tears before speaking.

"So, I want you to go down into the cellar and wait for just a little bit until I say it's okay to come out," she said. "It will be like playing hide and seek."

"You can do that for momma?" she asked.

The children cautiously nodded yes, and Jonas began leading them down the narrow steps. When they were all settled at the bottom of the cellar, their tearful faces looking up, Hannah slowly closed the door.

She turned from the cellar and ran crying to the house. When she reached the front door she heard two more shots.

"Oh my God," she said. "Something bad is happening!"

Hannah flung open the porch door and ran inside. She went to the kitchen and reached up, grabbing the shotgun from its pegs on the wall above the pantry door.

Then she went to the counter and opened the drawer where the ammunition was stored. Hannah loaded the shotgun and grabbed handfuls of shells, which she dumped in her apron pockets.

She walked to the window in the parlor and slowly pulled back the blanket. The prairie grass was almost still, with only a slight breeze. The cottonwoods in the shelter-belt stood quiet and motionless. The road leading to the farm was empty. There was nothing moving anywhere.

It's too quiet, she thought. *It's too still.*

Hannah felt a sudden urge to scream, breaking the awful silence, but she quickly covered her mouth. She must be very quiet, standing by the window, standing guard. Her only choice was to wait for someone to come, something to happen, but she did not know what.

Hannah was certain of only one thing. She would not cower. She would silently wait by the window, and she would shoot anyone who came to harm her children.

At that moment, Nils was three miles south of his farm, unaware of the fear that gripped Hannah and his children.

Nils smiled when the "big hill" came into view. As he drew nearer he could see the dirt road winding to the west around the base. The big hill wasn't actually that big; it was more of a wide and low mound rising above the prairie. Still it became a local landmark at the south-ern edge of Rainbow Valley. The valley, nearly indistin-guishable from the surrounding plains, spread out as flat as a tabletop, surrounded by other low hills.

As Nils and his team of horses continued down the road he could see the Sanderson farm up ahead. The new timber on the sides of the house seemed to shine in the sun.

In the distance he could see a bank of cumulous clouds forming far to the north, but the sky above him was clear. The air was fresh and warm, with only a gentle breeze. The only sound came from his horses' hooves clomping on road.

"Hey girls, what a fine day this is," Nils said, He often talked to his horses. One of horses whinnied back and Nils began to chuckle. He felt really good. His wagon was filled with their supplies. Soon he would arrive at the farm to be greeted by Hannah and the children. "Who could ask for anything more than that?" he asked his horses.

Nils began to whistle a tune; he could see the ears on his horses turning to listen. He chuckled again and then resumed whistling the tune, mostly to his horses.

As they passed the entrance to the Sanderson farm, there was a sudden change in the team of horses. Mollie, the oldest of the four, suddenly slowed her pace, disrupting the rhythm of the team. Then all the horses stopped and they all began to sniff the air. Nils looked at the horses and then at the Sanderson farm. The farm looked normal, but there was no movement anywhere. Nils, too, began to sense that something was wrong.

"What is it girls?" he asked his horses. They stood unmoving on the road, still sniffing the air. Then Nils heard the cry.

"Help, please help me." The cry was coming from somewhere on the farm.

Nils jumped down from the wagon and ran to the house.

As he neared the front door, he heard the cry again. "Help me, please!" The voice was coming from the barn. Nils ran to the barn and flung open the door. Lying on a floor was Otto Sanderson, his chest covered with blood.

"I've been shot," he said. Nils kneeled beside Otto and gently pulled back his shirt. Blood was oozing out of the bullet hole in the middle of his chest.

"Who did this?" Nils asked.

"Singleton," Otto said. "Singleton did it!" Otto screamed the words, which seemed to slice through the air. "We went to the barn to get some tools, and when I turned around he had a pistol pointed at me. And then he fired, just like that."

"Why?" Nils asked.

"I don't know," Otto said, slowly shaking his head. His eyes were wide with fear as he looked up at Nils. "After I fell to the ground I heard more shots," he said. "I think he may have shot Mabel and Lilly too."

Otto's voice broke, his eyes filled with tears and he began to sob. The tears spilled off his chin onto his bloody chest.

"Do you know where Mabel and Lilly are?" Nils asked.

"In the house," Otto whispered; then he began to sob again.

Nils ran out of the barn and to his wagon, retrieving his pistol from under the seat. His face was rigid as he approached the house. He wondered, *What horror might lie inside?* Nils cautiously pushed open the door.

As he stepped into the kitchen he saw Mabel's body sprawled face-down on the floor, a pool of blood surrounding her head. Nils dropped to one knee, keeping his pistol trained on the door to the parlor, and grasped Mabel's arm, feeling for a pulse. There was none.

He slowly stood and moved to the parlor. Stepping through the doorway, he saw that the room was empty.

"Hello," he called out. "Lilly, are you in here?"

There was only silence. He continued toward the bedroom door. As he neared the doorway he could see Lilly. She was lying on her back on the floor, her face covered with blood. Nils kneeled again to take her pulse, but there was none.

He quickly searched all areas of the house and then ran back to the barn.

"Did you find them?" Otto asked as he looked up at Nils.

"They're both dead," Nils said.

Otto's body shook, his face became twisted and he began to sob. "Oh, no, not my Mabel ... not my Lilly ..."

Nils looked down at Otto and tried to comfort him by gently holding his shoulders. "I'm sorry, Otto," he said. "I'm really sorry."

Nils brushed Otto's hair back from his forehead. "I'm going to take you down to our house," he said. "Hannah can treat your wound and try to stop the bleeding."

He moved behind Otto, slid his arms under his shoulder and began dragging him toward the wagon.

Otto's sobbing stopped and he began to moan in pain. When Nils reached the wagon, he laid Otto on the road and moved several sacks of seed at the rear of the wagon.

Nils kneeled down on the road, slid his arms under Otto's back and his legs and lifted him onto the wagon.

There was only a half-mile left to his farm, and now Nils was very anxious to get there.

"Come on, girls!" he shouted. "Let's go!" His horses began a fast trot, pulling the heavy wagon much more quickly down the road.

At the farm, Hannah was still standing guard at the window. She didn't know how long she had been standing there, but her legs were beginning to ache. Time seemed to be standing still, yet, when she looked to the shelterbelt the shadows of the cottonwoods were steadily moving to the east. It was probably late afternoon, she thought.

Normally at this time of day the youngest children would be outside playing after awakening from their naps. Now, the thought of her children cowering in fear in the root cellar was almost more than she could bear. She wanted to run to the cellar, throw open the door and embrace all of them, telling them everything was all right.

But, of course, she couldn't do that. At that moment, the safest place for her children was away from her and in the root cellar. The cellar was the one place on their farm that did not stand out in the bright prairie sun.

"It's the only place on this godforsaken land where they can hide," Hannah said. She spoke the words out loud to break the terrible silence in the parlor.

Unlike the hidden cellar, she knew the house did stand out. Its bright white exterior and the two stories attracted the attention of anyone passing through this part of Rainbow Valley.

And that is why Hannah waited in the house, ready to shoot any intruder. She would fight to the end. And even if she lost the battle, her children might still survive, hiding in the earth, away from her.

Suddenly Hannah saw something moving on the road. At first, her view was distorted by shimmering heat waves above the road. She stood perfectly still, focusing on the road, simultaneously pumping the shotgun so she could fire if need be.

Slowly the horses and wagon came clearly into view.

"It's Nils," she shouted. "He's coming home!"

She leaned the shotgun against the wall and ran out of the house. As the wagon approached, Hannah's smile quickly faded when she saw the grim expression on Nils' face.

"What's wrong?" she asked.

"The Sandersons have all been shot," Nils said. "Otto is in the back of the wagon." Nils stopped and jumped down from his seat and rushed to the back of the wagon.

Hannah stood motionless.

"They've all been shot?" she asked.

"All of them," Nils said. "Mabel and Lilly are dead, but now we must move Otto into the house and try to save him. He's bleeding bad."

They carried Otto inside and made their way to their bedroom where they lowered him onto their bed.

"I'll get some water so I can wash his wound," said Hannah as she rushed out of the room.

As she entered the parlor she stopped and picked the shotgun up from against the wall. It appeared as though she'd suddenly forgotten about treating Otto. Hannah walked to the window, grabbed the blanket and gave it a yank.

As the blanket fell to the floor Hannah pressed closer to the window and peered out. The road was empty; she could see no movement anywhere, but she must continue her guard.

"What are you doing in here?" Nils asked.

Hannah flinched at the sound of Nils' voice. "And where are the children?" he asked.

"The children are safe; they're hiding in the root cellar," she said. "But where is the man who shot Otto?"

Her hands were trembling as she stood holding the shotgun, but her eyes were cold and steady. Nils had never seen Hannah like this; she looked like she was ready to attack.

"Hannah, it's okay now," he said as he approached and lifted the shotgun from her hands, leaning it against the wall.

"I think the shooter is gone," Nils added. He wrapped his arms around her and pulled her to his chest. Hannah's rigid body seemed to soften and she began to cry.

"Oh, Nils," she sobbed, "I'm frightened. I thought we

were all going to die. I heard the shots and gathered the children, but there was *no place* to hide. And then I remembered the root cellar."

There was an awkward pause in her voice. "The children, oh my God, the children. They're still in the cellar. They must be scared to death!"

"I'll go get the children while you tend to Otto," Nils said as he rushed out of the house. When he reached the root cellar he opened the door and began lifting the children out one by one as they climbed up the ladder.

Nils dropped to his knees and embraced the children, wiping the tears from their faces.

"It's all right now," Nils announced. "We're all safe."

"We must all go into the house now," he added. "But you must stay out of our bedroom. Otto Sanderson is sick and we're treating him in there."

The children nodded and followed him to the house.

When they reached the door, Nils tapped Jonas on the shoulder and motioned for him to step aside. He waited until the other children had gone into the house.

"I want you to saddle up Mollie and ride over to Glenn Heggen's farm," he said. "Tell Glenn they must send someone to town to summon both the police chief and doctor to our house."

Jonas' eyes were growing wide, and a confused look was spreading across his face.

"Otto Sanderson has been shot and is barely hanging on," Nils said. "Mabel and Lilly were also shot and they're both dead. Tell them the shooter is John Singleton, the Sanderson's hired hand, and he's still on the loose."

Nils paused and shook his head. He felt terrible reciting the gruesome details to his 10-year-old son.

"So that's why we need the police chief and doctor here as quickly as possible," Nils said. "The Heggens have the best horses in the valley; they can ride to town faster than anyone."

Jonas' nodded at his father. His eyes were still open wide, but the confused look was fading.

Jonas turned and ran to the barn. A few minutes later he led Mollie to the front of the house and swung up into the saddle.

Nils came outside, patted Mollie on her neck and looked up. Jonas noticed there were blood stains on his father's shirtsleeves.

"One last thing," Nils said. "If you see any man walking on the road, or crossing a field, you must turn Mollie around and ride back here as fast as possible."

Jonas nodded down to his father. He looked very small sitting up there on such a large horse. Jonas trotted Mollie out to the road, and they disappeared behind the shelterbelt. Nils stood and listened, then he heard Mollie's hoofs pounding down the road in a full gallop.

Nils hurried back into the house to help Hannah treat Otto. She had removed his shirt and was cleaning the area around the bullet wound. A pile of gauze and bottles from their medicine drawer were spread out on the table next to the bed.

Hannah began applying the gauze to the chest wound.

Then Nils lifted Otto's torso from the bed so Hannah could begin wrapping a torn bed sheet around his body. Otto moaned as Hannah pulled the sheet tightly to hold the gauze against the wound.

"He's drifting in and out of consciousness," she said. "But at least I think we can stop the bleeding."

Later that day the police chief and doctor arrived at the Berge farm. The doctor removed the bullet from Otto's chest, and later, when Otto regained consciousness, the police chief asked him to tell everything that happened. Meanwhile, the farmers in Rainbow Valley organized a posse and began scouring the land, looking for John Singleton.

The following morning, Otto Sanderson died. The doctor shook his head as he pulled the sheet over Otto's face. When he turned to Hannah, she saw a knowing look on his face; this doctor had obviously treated gunshot wounds before.

"I'm surprised he lasted this long," the doctor said. "The wound was severe and things were torn to hell inside him. He must have been shot at very close range."

Two days after the murders, Singleton was arrested at the railroad station in Ray. The young man was sitting on a bench, waiting for the eastbound train, when the police took him into custody.

Singleton was taken to the town jail, where the police chief began to question him. Singleton denied killing the Sandersons, but when the chief searched his pockets he found a large amount of cash and two rings.

The following day, Mabel Sanderson's sister arrived

at the jail. The police chief led the sister into his office, opened a brown envelope and dropped the rings onto the felt pad on his desktop.

The sister leaned forward and closely examined the rings. Tears began spilling off her cheeks, leaving wet markings in the felt.

"Yes," she whispered, raising her head to look at the chief. "Those are Mabel and Otto's wedding rings."

"You're sure?" he asked.

"Yes, I'm positive" the sister replied. "I was in their wedding."

Later that day, when told of the ring identification, Singleton confessed to the three murders.

When the police chief asked him why he did it, the young man only shrugged his shoulders. "I was broke and I needed money," he said.

The chief shook his head, a look of anguish and disgust on his face, and led Singleton back to his jail cell. Then he sent a message to the district attorney in Williston, stating John Singleton had confessed to committing the murders. The police chief said he and another officer would transport Singleton to the county courthouse and turn him over to the sheriff.

Three days later, Singleton stood before the judge for his arraignment in district court in Williston. The courtroom was packed with spectators. The murder charges were formally read and Singleton was asked, "How do you plead?"

"Guilty, your honor," Singleton said.

Chaos erupted in the courtroom, and there were angry shouts and jeers. The havoc grew louder as the crowd surged forward, overturning desks and chairs as they moved toward Singleton.

"Murderer," someone shouted above the noise of the crowd. "You're a dirty murderer!"

The judge repeatedly banged his gavel on his desk, but no one heard or even noticed. The angry crowd was focused only on Singleton.

As the crowd surged closer, a side door suddenly opened and three sheriff's deputies rushed in, grabbing Singleton up from his chair. One officer dragged Singleton back through the door. The two other deputies slammed the door shut, locked it and turned to face the angry crowd.

"Move back!" they shouted. Both raised their batons.

The judge and his court stenographer looked down at the mayhem. "Order!" the judge shouted, waving his gavel in the air. "Order in this courtroom!"

The angry crowd turned from the deputies and spilled out into the hallway. More deputies appeared at the end of the hall, rushed forward and began pushing the crowd back toward the front of the building. When the crowd was forced outside, deputies locked the front door and stood guard, their weapons ready.

Back in the courtroom, the judge and his stenographer made their way through the overturned desks and chairs and walked out into the hallway. The judge paused at the doorway when he noticed he was still carrying his gavel. He dropped the gavel in the front pocket of his robe and approached the deputies.

"I've never seen such anger in my court," the judge said. "Thank God you acted so quickly."

That evening, around 8 p.m., the sheriff received a report of a shooting at Stockman's Bar, three miles west of Williston. There were also reports that an unruly crowd was gathering outside the bar and that several fights were erupting.

The sheriff, needing as many officers as possible to control the mob, set out with three of his deputies, leaving one deputy at the jail.

As soon as the sheriff and his deputies left, a group of masked men arrived at the jail, rushing through the front door. Their plan was working perfectly.

The lone officer saw the approaching mob and grabbed the keys to the jail cells. He ran to the end of the hallway, entered a small cell and locked himself in. Then he pulled out his pistol and waited.

"I'll shoot anyone trying to get into this cell," he shouted. "I order all of you to get out of this building, now!"

The masked men ignored the officer, going instead to Singleton's cell. They carried several large crow bars. In just a few minutes they were able to pry open the cell door.

The first man rushing into the cell smashed his fist into Singleton's face, sending Singleton flying backwards onto his bunk.

Several other men pounced on the fallen man, kicking

and punching him. Then they dragged him from the cell.

Singleton's hands were tied behind his back, and the men took him outside. They lifted him up and tossed him into the back of a wagon. The mob was moving with cold precision; they looked like they were nonchalantly tossing a bag of potatoes in the wagon.

A few minutes later, the crowd arrived at the small bridge crossing the Little Muddy River on the east side of Williston. A full moon was rising above the eastern hills, casting a surreal light on the bridge while the sun began to set in the west. Singleton was pulled from the wagon, landing hard on the ground. A rope was fastened around his neck, and the men pushed him forward to the middle of the bridge.

Two men waited in the middle, looking down at the water, trying to determine the distance. Then they measured the rope and tied one end to the bridge. The crowd grew strangely quiet as they watched Singleton struggle with the men as they lifted him over the bridge railing to a narrow ledge. Singleton stood very still, the noose around his neck, trying to balance himself on the ledge. The moon was reflected on the water below him. The eerie silence was suddenly broken by a low moaning sound. Singleton was sobbing.

One of the men stepped to the railing, reached over and pushed Singleton from the ledge. As Singleton fell forward the rope tightened, snapping his body backward as his legs plunged into the water up to his knees.

His legs began thrashing in the water as the rope tightened, slowly strangling him. The frantic thrashing motion began to slow and Singleton's body became still.

A shot rang out, whirling the body around from the force of impact. Then several more shots were fired.

"Shoot that son of a bitch full of lead," someone shouted. "Just in case …"

More shots rang out and then suddenly it was quiet.

"Let's get out of here before the sheriff comes," someone shouted.

The crowd quickly dispersed, leaving Singleton's lifeless body suspended from the bridge, the bottoms of his legs immersed in the water. The smell of gunfire lingered in the night air. The Little Muddy continued its gentle flow under the bridge, moving toward its nearby confluence with the Missouri River. An eddy moved down the stream, slowly twirling the hanged man's body in the current. Then the eddy passed and everything was still once again.

———·——   ——··——

"It's time for dinner," their mother called. She entered the parlor and went to help Bestefar up from his chair.

Eric and his sisters lingered on the sofa. Their mother saw the spellbound looks on their faces and turned to Bestefar.

"Did you tell them another one of your stories from the old days?" she asked.

"Ja, I told them about the Sanderson murders," Bestefar said.

"Uff da," their mother said. "That's not a very good story to hear before dinner."

Bestefar shrugged his shoulders. "Well, it happened," he said.

Seated at the dinner table, Eric looked at his plate of roast beef, mashed potatoes and peas. The food smelled delicious, but he was not hungry.

He lifted his eyes from his plate and looked at Bestefar, sitting at the far end of the table. Bestefar and the other adults were laughing as they ate their dinner, talking in their usual linguistic mix of English and Norwegian.

Eric couldn't stop staring at his grandfather. For the first time in his life, Eric saw him in a very different light. This elderly Norse had experienced so many things, both good and bad.

He had seen life come into the world, including a son and daughter sitting with him at this dinner table. And he had seen a life taken when Otto Sanderson lay sobbing and then dying on his bed.

Bestefar's new life in America was not without turmoil, but he had endured, and his six children and 15 grandchildren now traced part of their roots back to this one man. When Eric looked at Bestefar, he also saw a part of himself.

Bestefar sat happily at the head of the table, celebrating his life. He'd faced many dangers and challenges in his 90 years, including the bear that charged him on a mountain trail. Bestefar, the superstitious Nordic, shot the bear and removed the bullet from the carcass, carrying the slug in his pocket for the rest of his life. It sounded like an ancient legend from Norse mythology: a bear is sacrificed to bring a man good luck.

Other challenges that Bestefar faced were more lasting. He was only 21 years old when he decided to leave Norway to begin a new life in a strange land. He left his parents, six brothers and two sisters standing on the pier. They were all crying as they watched him board the ship. He waved goodbye and never saw any of them again.

In the "New World," Bestefar staked his homestead claim on the empty prairie. Hannah joined him and they plowed the earth and planted their seeds. They began raising their family while surviving winter blizzards, summer droughts, roughshod cowboys, wandering thieves and one cold-hearted murderer.

Bestefar had often struggled to survive on the prairie, and he had won.

And now, on this special day, Bestefar sat smiling, laughing and speaking mostly in Norwegian. The Norse king still ruled his subjects. He looked content, like he'd done everything he had set out to do.

Chapter 6

Different Cultures

The northern Great Plains are home to two diverse groups of people, the Indians and the descendants of European immigrants.

The Indians, of course, were the first to arrive. Thousands of years ago they began migrating from Asia to North America via a land bridge that once linked the two continents.

As the Indians migrated south to the Great Plains, several tribes evolved different ways of life. The nomadic tribes constantly followed vast herds of buffalo. The buffalo provided everything — food, hides for clothing and tents, and even bones for tools and knives. Other tribes were more stationary and lived in villages. Although they also hunted buffalo, they raised crops as well.

All of the Plains Indians felt blessed to live in such a bountiful place. The endless prairie, stretching from horizon to horizon, provided everything they needed. They were thankful and very spiritual, believing the Great Spirit had power over all things on the plains. They sensed the Spirit's presence wherever they went.

For many centuries, the Indians were the sole inhabitants of this land. They called themselves "the people," and it seemed their way of life would endure forever.

In the 1800s, however, white settlers began moving

west. The wagon trains lumbered westward, but most did not stop to settle the Great Plains, which were still labeled the "Great American Desert" on maps. The semi-arid land, stretching for hundreds of miles from the Rocky Mountains to the east, looked too forbidding. The prairie was a place to be crossed, not settled. So the wagon trains continued on to better land in the Far West.

As more settlers moved to the Far West, however, much of the good land there was taken. Suddenly the Great Plains didn't look so forbidding. A new westward expansion began, but this time the migrants were going to settle on the Great Plains rather than cross it.

For the arriving settlers, the land looked somewhat monotonous, a sea of grass, often without a tree in sight. But they soon discovered the Great Plains were hiding an incredible treasure just below the surface.

The settlers often found incredibly rich topsoil that lay undisturbed for millennia, nurtured by nature and the massive herds of buffalo grazing its surface. Even more astounding, when they dug deeper into the earth, they were amazed at the depth of the topsoil, which reached several feet in some areas.

Huge swaths of the northern Great Plains were now destined to become farmland; much of this change to the landscape would be done by immigrants from Europe who were unfamiliar with the land.

Nothing like the Great Plains existed anywhere in Europe, and when the immigrants looked out on the endless prairie, it often looked unsettling to them. To them, the prairie looked wild and untamed, something that must be controlled. They decided they would change the land, the very lifeblood of the prairie.

The European immigrants' carefully calculated plans left little room for any spiritual connection to the prairie. In contrast, the Plains Indians revered the land as almost sacred. The Indians believed that the Great Spirit had power over everything and that all things possessed spirits. The earth was the mother of all spirits.

The Plains Indians' spirituality was tied to the land itself, but the Europeans saved their spirituality for Sunday services inside the churches they built.

For some Europeans, the prairie looked strange and uninviting. Some were so unnerved when they first looked out over Great Plains that they turned and left. Others reluctantly decided to stay, but they would never feel at home on the prairie. Many of them secretly hated the land.

"Give it back to the Indians" became common slang among settlers when they grew tired of life on the prairie, a place where summer heat can equal the Sahara and winter nights can be as cold as the Arctic.

However, despite the extreme weather and other hardships, most decided to stay. They built their houses of sod, plowed the prairie and seeded their fields with grain. Their life was often hard, enduring winter blizzards and summer droughts. Massive clouds of locusts, so dense they darkened the sky, sometimes swept down onto the land, eating every kernel of grain in their fields. The settlers could do nothing but watch their year-long labor be devoured by giant insects. And then they wondered how they'd feed their families. How would they survive?

They lived their lives in constant struggle and the fear of going bankrupt and losing their farms. Unknown to them, they were evolving into their own unique culture. The settlers that succeeded were certain that *their* way was the only way to survive on this new land. The prairie was molding these survivors into the most stubborn people on earth.

A new culture took root on the prairie. The settlers'· children, born in sod houses to shelter them from the summer heat and winter cold, considered their lives entirely normal. They knew of nothing else. They did not find it particularly alarming if a clump of dirt fell onto the super table. Or if a rattlesnake slithered across the pathway as they walked to the barn.

At night, the settler's children listened in awe as their parents told bedtime stories of their life back in "the old country." As they listened, the children tried to imagine what Europe looked like. But all they could picture was a foreign place, much different from the Great Plains. And when their parents talked of their lives in the old country, they secretly thanked their parents for leaving Europe and coming here.

On the Northern Plains, General George Armstrong Custer "cleared" much of the land of Indians before the immigrants arrived. Huge sections of the Dakotas were opened to settlement under the government's Homestead Act. After paying a nominal filing fee and agreeing to live on the land as ranchers or farmers, homesteaders were granted 160-acre parcels by the U.S. government.

The Homestead Act brought more than 100,000 people to the northern part of Dakota Territory between 1879 and 1886. On the eve of statehood in November 1889, North Dakota still had 21 million acres of land available for homesteading.

Papers in hand, the homesteaders set out in their new land. One can only imagine their thoughts as they drove their horses and wagons across the endless prairie. There were few landmarks, other than an occasional farm. The farms looked lonely, sitting on the prairie, the low-slung sod homes half hidden by the tall native grass.

The land seemed almost lifeless, other than an occasional antelope suddenly leaping out of the grass, or a pheasant flapping up to the sky. The only other movement on the plains was the grass itself, pushed by the wind in waves across the rolling hills. To the Europeans, the flowing grass looked strangely familiar, much like the ocean waves on their trans-Atlantic crossings.

There was one other thing the settlers noticed as they first made their way to their land. The prairie was almost silent. The creaking of their wagons and beating of their horses' hooves on the ground were the only sounds they heard. Many settlers found no pleasure in this quiet. They longed to hear even a single chirp from a bird.

But others shrugged at the stillness on the prairie and they would break into loud, joyful folksongs from the homeland. For these settlers, the lonely quietness of the prairie offered a new freedom. They could sing at the top of their lungs, even missing a note, and there was no one to criticize them.

When the settlers finally arrived at their 160-acre parcels, they stopped and looked closer at the land. Now the land appeared more intimate, almost nestled under the big sky. Reaching down, they traditionally pulled a clump of prairie grass and examined the dirt surrounding the roots. The soil was dark and smelled good, a loamy mixture that would bring a smile to the homesteaders' faces. This soil was rich, and now it was *their* soil.

This ritual for was played over and over by countless homesteaders, many of whom were immigrants from Norway, including Eric's grandparents, who homesteaded in North Dakota in the early 1900s.

Norwegians love to tell stories, and the stories they told often had two parts: They told of their "first life" in Norway and then transitioned to their "new life" in Dakota.

They described the tall, thick buffalo grass, which covered the land when they first arrived. The thick grass provided abundant feed for their livestock, but it also became fuel for deadly prairie fires. The fires sometimes spread for miles, consuming everything in their path. Grain fields erupted in the inferno and cattle and horses were sometimes burned alive as they ran through the flames, trying to find a way out. The settlers and their families fled for their lives, but occasionally some of them met terrible deaths as well.

But of all their grandparents' stories, the most disturbing were of Indian massacres of settlers, which occurred years earlier in Minnesota. Entire families of settlers were slaughtered by screaming warriors.

Fortunately, their grandparents said there were few Indian conflicts in this part of North Dakota. In fact, they seldom saw any Indians, even in the early days of their homesteads. Most Indians had been moved onto reservations, and there were only small bands of Plains Indians that occasionally passed by their farm.

Sometimes the Indians would stop and stare at the dugout, and they would shake their heads when the Eric's grandparents spoke Norwegian to them. If the Indians spotted the vegetable garden nearby, they would dismount from their horses to pick vegetables, never asking for permission to do so.

At first, Eric's grandparents reacted with surprise and anger. *Damn, thieving Indians,* they thought. But they soon grudgingly accepted this behavior when they learned more of Indian traditions. Some nomadic tribes, they learned, believed that whatever grew on the prairie belonged to everyone who lived there.

In addition to the cultural differences, the encounters between homesteaders and Indians were awkward because both groups now considered the prairie *their* land. Two groups now called Dakota home, but they were as different as night and day, contrasting cultures that might never blend.

The cultural divide was further enforced by government bureaucrats who marked boundaries across the prairie. Brown people lived mostly on reservations and white people lived everywhere else.

By the early 1900s, the Indians seemed to almost disappear from the land, while growing numbers of Europeans and other settlers continued to arrive. Years earlier, the Indians had watched helplessly as the white men slaughtered the buffalo until the giant herds vanished from the land. And now the white man forced the Indians onto this new reservation land, detached from the settlers. It seemed unthinkable to the Indians that this could happen, but it did.

With the buffalo gone and the Indians moved to reservations, the homesteaders built their farms, ranches and towns. They graded dirt roads and laid railroad tracks across the Great Plains. The native grass was plowed into the earth and replaced by immense fields of wheat and barley.

The Great Plains were changed forever. The only thing that would remain the same was the immense sky above and the wind that would flow across this land forever.

—·—   —·—

Olaf Halvorson was a grandson of Norwegian homesteaders. When his father turned 70 years old, Olaf inherited his 2,000-acre farm.

The Halvorson family farm sat at the bottom of a small valley in the hills about five miles west of Alexander. The shingled farmhouse had two stories and faced south toward a corral and small red barn. At the rear of the house was a large garden. A shelterbelt with several rows of trees bordered the northern edge of the farm, providing a buffer from the winds that swept down the valley.

A narrow dirt road stretched a quarter mile from the farmhouse out to the county road, which was graveled.

As the school year neared an end, Olaf offered Eric, who was now 15 years old, a summer job as his hired hand. The pay wasn't much, $10 a day, but it included the usual room and board and one day off each week, which was Sunday. The only exception to this schedule would come during harvest at the end of summer when they would work seven days a week.

Eric's work would include driving tractor to plow weeds in the summer-fallow fields. He would also feed the cows, stack hay and mend the fences surrounding the pastures. This was Eric's first summer job on a farm.

When Eric first met Olaf and his wife, Julia, he thought they were a nice couple. The Halvorsons were young newlyweds and acted much differently than most couples that Eric knew.

Olaf stood tall and muscular with reddish-blond hair, a square jaw and dark blue eyes. Julia was tall and slim, her blond hair falling to her shoulders. Like her husband, Julia's Nordic eyes were dark blue. Her lips were full and seemed set in a perpetual smile.

The first time Eric saw Julia up close, he couldn't stop staring. She was the most beautiful woman he had ever seen. And now he could hardly believe his good luck since he would be living in Julia's house for the summer.

"Uff da," Julia pinched her nose as Olaf and Eric entered the kitchen after Eric's first day of work on the farm. "You need a shower if you want to eat super with me."

Olaf laughed and slapped Julia's bottom as he brushed

by. Julia ran after him and swatted Olaf's buttocks, prompting an outburst of laughter. Olaf lifted Julia fully off the floor and held her against the wall as they embraced.

"Uff da, I mean it," Julia said as Olaf loosened his grip. "You stink."

Supper that night included mashed potatoes, roast beef, and carrots and peas, freshly picked from the garden.

The farmhouse was still warm from the day's heat; Julia filled their glasses with iced tea to wash down the food.

When they finished eating they lingered at the kitchen table and talked. Eric noticed that even as they talked, Olaf and Julia were holding hands under the table, smiling.

Eric was mesmerized by the Halvorsons. The young couple was different from most Scandinavians, who tend not to show their emotions before others. The Halvorsons, however, seemed uninhibited. It was obvious they were in love; they were like an open book.

When Eric realized he was staring at them, his face flushed and he started to get up from the table.

Julia slid her hand across the table, resting it on Eric's arm. It almost startled him, but then he looked at Julia's blue eyes and settled back in his chair.

"I heard about your horse accident," Julia said. "I'm really sorry. I know what it's like to lose a horse."

Eric nodded, but didn't speak.

"When I was 10 years old I had a pinto named Flicker,"

Julia said, the smile suddenly fading from her lips. "We were riding one day when Flicker stepped in a gopher hole and broke her leg." She paused and sighed softly. "My dad had to shoot her to put her out of her misery."

Julia's eyes were turning moist, but she continued talking in a steady voice. "I really thought my world was going to end right there," she said. "But, of course, my world didn't end. Now I only think of all those wonderful days when Flicker and I rode happily across the prairie."

She paused as if to catch her breath, still staring directly into Eric's face. "I know Flicker is in horse heaven, wherever that is." The smile had returned to Julia's lips as she squeezed Eric's arm.

She's not just beautiful on the outside, Eric thought. *She's beautiful right down to the core.*

Eric was so mesmerized that he didn't realize that the room had grown silent. Julia was waiting for a response. He moved a little in his chair before speaking.

"I miss Moonlight a lot," Eric said. His face tightened as he searched for more words. "She was good horse," he said, almost in a whisper. "We had a lot of fun together."

Eric's eyes were staring at the floor as he spoke. Then he raised his head and looked at Julia again, forcing a smile to his lips. "But, like you say, Moonlight is probably up there in horse heaven right now, eating alfalfa with Flicker."

They all laughed loudly, and Olaf reached across the table to grip Eric's shoulder, giving it a friendly squeeze.

The upstairs bedrooms were still warm when they

went up to bed later that night, but a slight breeze was stirring outside, and the curtains on the open windows were beginning to move slightly.

Eric went to his room and sat on the edge of his bed, stretching his legs. He was tired after driving the tractor all day, circling a large field and plowing the weeds into the ground.

He stood and walked to the window and pulled the curtains to the side. Heat lightning was starting to build up far to the west, with faint purple flashes across the horizon. A group of coyotes suddenly howled in the hills above the barn, and then they fell silent.

Eric leaned out of his window to look up at the bright stars. The night air was warm and friendly, much different from the harsh, bright heat of the day. The stars spread all the way to the horizon, where the flashes of heat lightning continued.

He pulled back inside the window and decided to get ready for bed. He grabbed his toothbrush from the tray on the dresser, stepped out of his room into the darkened hallway and began walking to the bathroom. As he neared the bathroom a slice of light stretched across the doorway from the Halvorson's bedroom. The door was open just a few inches.

As he passed, Eric glanced at the opening in the doorway. Julia and Olaf lay naked on the bed, their bodies moving together in a rhythmic motion.

Oh my God, Eric thought. *They're doing it!*

Julia's moans were growing louder as Eric turned in the hallway and began quietly walking back to his room.

His eyes were open wide as he made his way through the darkness. When he reached his doorway he slowly pushed it open, careful not to make any noise. Julia's moans filled the hallway behind him as Eric stepped into his bedroom and closed the door.

He went to the dresser and laid his toothbrush on the tray. Then he sat on the edge of his bed, staring out the window at the stars.

A smile formed on Eric's face as he lay back on his bed. He felt warm, natural and intimate, much like the soft night air outside his window; much like the lovers down the hall. It all seemed to flow together on this warm Dakota night.

Eric would remember this night, and this feeling, forever.

Eric soon discovered the monotony of working on a farm. After a 12-hour day in the field, his skin was dry and burned, his muscles tired and his mind eager for anything not related to agriculture.

Farm work could be hard, and it could be tedious. On this particular day, Eric was driving a tractor that pulled a cultivator, which churned the weeds into the ground, turning the entire field a solid mass of brown. This process was called "summer fallowing" in which farm land was purposely kept out of production to help rebuild soil and conserve moisture for the next season.

Eric sat on the tractor, circling the 80-acre field. It

would be a tedious day, circling the big field, slowly moving closer to the center. As he turned the tractor at the corner of the field, he thought he saw some movement in the taller weeds near the middle of the 80 acres. He stared at the middle, but the grass and weeds were still.

His tractor continued to circle the field, churning the earth and slowly moving closer to the center. Suddenly Eric caught the movement again out of the corner of his eye. Then he spotted the antelope standing in the weeds 100 yards from him. At the side of the antelope stood her little calf.

Suddenly the tractor lurched upward, bouncing Eric in his seat. He had steered off course and the tractor was bouncing directly across the furrows. Eric stopped the tractor, turned off the ignition and jumped down to the ground. He needed a break, anyway, from this tedium. Picking up a clod of dirt he tossed it high in the sky. The clod sailed through the air then fell onto the plowed earth, creating a small cloud of dust that drifted away with the wind. Eric reached for the water bag behind the seat and took a long drink. The water was still slightly cool and refreshing to taste.

He walked to the front of the tractor and looked to the center of the field where the antelope still stood, her calf at her side. The antelope dropped her head and appeared to be nudging the calf.

Eric climbed back onto the tractor, looked out over the field and sighed.

I'll probably still be plowing this dumb field tomorrow, he thought. He looked up at the warm sun and cloudless sky and shook his head. *Just another day on the prairie, with nothing changing except the recent arrival of one new antelope,* he thought.

He flipped the switch, and the tractor engine spurted to life. Dropping it in gear, he made a small loop and straightened the wheels as the tractor turned into the row of plowed earth. He began following the monotonous line, cultivating the field.

On days like this, when farm work grew really tedious and boring, Eric's mind began to wander. He would think of Moonlight and their rides up to Ragged Butte and their swims at Jackson Lake. He wondered if any of his friends would be swimming at Lonesome Lagoon on this warm day. He thought of diving into the cool water and floating in the middle of the lagoon.

And he thought of Julia, the most beautiful woman in the world, who cooked his meals, made friendly conversation at the super table and lay naked on her bed at night.

An hour passed before Eric ended his daydreaming. His mouth was parched and he reached behind the seat, grabbed the water beg and took another long drink. Wiping his lips, he capped the bag and put it back on the hook. The day was becoming hot as the sun beat down on the plains.

He glanced to the middle of the field where the antelope and her calf still stood. The antelope was circling her calf, looking nervous as the tractor slowly edged closer.

As Eric neared the corner of the field and turned the tractor, the antelope suddenly broke into a full run. She raced across the cultivated part of the field, her tiny calf close at her heels.

Eric stopped the tractor and stared in astonishment as the two ran off the field and disappeared over a small hill.

That little guy couldn't have been very old, maybe just a day or two, he thought. *And he ran as fast as his mother!*

Eric shook his head as he marveled at what he had just seen. Then he looked to the distant hills beyond the field. The afternoon sky had turned pale blue, and there still was not a cloud in sight.

With the antelope and her calf gone, the land seemed empty again. Eric felt like he was all alone in the world, sitting on the tractor under the big sky. He knew, of course, there were creatures out there on the prairie, gophers, prairie dogs and rattlesnakes. You just couldn't see them as they sheltered themselves in their cool underground burrows from the heat of the day.

It seemed as though only Eric was foolish enough to stay out in the burning sun on this hot day.

Eric glanced at the wooded coulees and imagined there could be fox, coyote or deer resting in the shade of the scrub trees and bushes. But then he eliminated the coyote from his imaginary list. If there was a coyote anywhere nearby, it would have seen the calf at the side of the mother antelope. The coyote would have stalked the antelope, perhaps hiding in the grass and then suddenly leaping out to kill the calf.

Eric thought about all the hidden creatures and realized that everything on the prairie evolved with its own methods of survival. For the newborn antelope, this meant it must run like an adult, only days after being born.

Eric couldn't stop thinking about the baby antelope as he restarted the tractor. He shook his head and almost frowned as he searched the empty prairie once again, looking for any movement. There was none. He was all alone.

This really is a hard, unforgiving land, he thought. *Uff da.*

Eric awakened to an ear-shattering clap of thunder, which shook his room so hard the window rattled.

He quickly dressed and went downstairs. Olaf and Julia were having coffee at the kitchen table.

Another loud boom shook the house, and a flash of lightning lit up the kitchen.

"Uff da," Julia said. "I don't like these storms."

"Well, we could use some rain on the wheat and barley fields," Olaf said, sipping his coffee. "And the hayfield on the south forty is getting pretty dry."

Julia sighed in agreement as she stood at the kitchen sink, peering out at the cottonwoods, which were bent by the wind and rain. "Well, as long as it doesn't hail," she said. "That would be bad."

Another loud clap of thunder shook the house. Olaf stood and walked to Julia, placing his arm around her waist as the two looked out the kitchen window at the storm.

Julia turned when she heard Eric sliding his chair into

the table.

"What do you want for breakfast, Eric?' Julia stood smiling down at him, smoothing her hair back on the side.

"Got eggs and bacon?" Eric asked.

"You betcha," Julia said smiling. "Coming right up."

By the time they finished eating breakfast, the storm was passing. As Eric got up from the table, rays of sunlight suddenly streamed through the window. It was a typical summer storm in the Dakotas, disappearing as quickly as it had arrived.

"Today I think today we'll saddle the horses and ride up past the Johnson place and check the fences in the north pasture," Olaf said. "I haven't been up there for a while."

Eric nodded and excitedly bounded up the stairs to go to the bathroom before they left.

"We could drive the jeep up there," Olaf said, as the two walked to the barn. "But you can't always follow the fence as good with a jeep as you can with a horse."

When they approached the horses, Olaf looked down at Eric, smiling. "Which one do you want to ride?"

Eric eyed the two mares, one black and the other brown in color. "I guess I'll take her," Eric said, as he approached the black mare, reaching up to stroke her mane. "What's her name?"

"Her name is Cody," Olaf said. "I'll be riding Sadie."

They rode single file, Olaf in front, on a narrow path that stretched north from the farm. The trail was at the bottom of a low valley. Eric smiled as they rode; it felt good to be on a horse again.

"Olaf, do you mind if I ride ahead for a bit?" Eric asked. "I think Cody wants to go for a little run."

Olaf nodded yes and Eric tapped his heels on Cody's side. "Let's go girl."

Cody broke into a gallop up the trail. As they gained full speed, Eric sat up straight in the saddle to feel the air rushing against his face, a smile forming on his lips. Eric's body was moving in perfect unison with Cody as they galloped down the trail.

They rode fast for a half mile before Eric felt Cody's rhythm begin to slow. He placed his hand on the side of her neck, which was wet.

"Whoa, girl," Eric said. "Let's slow down a bit." Cody slowed to a trot, then to a fast walk as they continued on the trail. Eric turned Cody off the trail toward a nearby creek bed. They followed the creek bed for a hundred yards before finding a single pool of water. They stopped and Cody drank, periodically raising her head and turning toward Eric, as if to say thanks.

"You're welcome," Eric said smiling. He liked this horse.

A few minutes later Olaf and Sadie rode up and stopped at the pool. The horses nuzzled each other, and Sadie took a long drink.

Reaching the north pasture, they began following the fence line, looking for areas of the fence that needed repair. The day had turned blistering hot; the sky was cloudless and the wind unusually calm.

They stopped several times to repair the fence, tightening loose wire and hammering it securely to the wooden posts. After several stops, the repairs began to feel almost tedious to Eric, like so many other jobs on the farm.

But today was different, he reminded himself. After each repair, Eric returned to his horse and climbed up in the saddle and they continued to follow the fence line.

It feels good to be in the saddle, Eric thought. *It's a lot better than sitting on a tractor all day.*

They stopped for lunch under a cottonwood tree next to the dry creek bed. Olaf lifted a pack from behind his saddle and walked to a shady spot under the tree. He kicked a couple rocks out of the way and sat down on the grass. "Let's see what Julia packed for us today," he said.

He pulled two large roast beef sandwiches from the pack, handing one to Eric. Then he reached back in the pack and pulled out two bags of potato chips. They ate in silence; the only sound was their munching.

Eric walked to his horse and got his water bag and returned to the shady spot. He took a long drink and offered the bag to Olaf.

"No thanks," Olaf said. "I've got some coffee in a thermos." He poured himself a cup and slurped it. "They say it's good to drink something hot on a hot day," he smiled. "Want some?"

"No thanks," Eric said as he continued to eat his sandwich.

Olaf was half reclined on the grass, sipping another

cup of coffee. He turned toward Eric and asked, "So tell me, what you're going to do when you grow up?"

Eric swallowed a mouthful of sandwich and took another drink of water. "Well, I really don't know," he said. "I haven't thought too much about it."

Olaf shrugged and his face turned more serious. "When I was a boy, I didn't think much either about what I was going to do. Then my dad started talking to me about taking over this farm."

"And now I own all this," Olaf said. He waved his arm in a broad sweep. "I own the whole damn thing."

"I don't know if that's a good thing or not," Olaf added, a wide grin on his face. "If Julia and I can make some money on this farm, then I guess it will be a good thing. But if we don't ..."

Olaf sighed and laid flat on the ground, pulling his cowboy hat over his face. "Time for a little snooze," he said, his voice trailing off.

Eric reclined halfway, resting on his elbow as he looked out on the valley. Meadow larks were calling to each other in the bushes above the dry creek.

What will I do when I grow up? Eric asked himself. *Maybe I'll be a doctor, a veterinarian, a cowboy?* He shook his head from side to side. He had no idea what he might do.

There was only one thing that was certain to Eric. He knew whatever he ended up doing in life he would do it here on the prairie. He couldn't imagine living anywhere else.

After all, the Dakotas were "the breadbasket of the

world," and that made this land special. And when he thought of living anywhere else, such as a city, he shuddered. He remembered a train trip he took with his father to Minneapolis. The downtown streets were crowded and noisy, and the air smelled funny. After they boarded the train to return to North Dakota, the train wound its way across the Minnesota countryside. Eric looked out the train window, shaking his head at the trees and lakes. He did not see any wide-open prairie anywhere. "Minnesota is ugly," he told his friends when he returned home.

Eric awakened when he heard Olaf lifting the pack back on his horse. Eric stood, wondering how long he had slept. Probably not long, he thought, but he still felt refreshed. He grabbed the water bag and climbed up in the saddle.

It was midafternoon when they finished following the fence line to the point where they had started that morning. The sun was becoming hotter and the air thick and still. As they rode down the trail toward the farm, Eric noticed the meadowlarks were no longer calling to each in the bushes above the creek bed.

The dry air seemed to parch his throat and Eric's arms were burned from the sun. The only sign of any relief from the furnace-like heat was a line of cumulous clouds forming far to the west, their tops billowing high above the horizon.

"I think we'll just ride home and call it a day," Olaf said. "It's too damn hot to work anymore today."

An hour later they rode into the farm, unsaddled the horses and put the fencing tools away in the barn.

"Hey Julia, we're back," Olaf called as they walked into the house. There was no response so Olaf went into the living room and looked out the window facing the garden. He smiled when he spotted Julia stooped over her vegetables.

Olaf grabbed a beer from the fridge. "You want a soda, Eric?" he asked.

"Sure, I'll have a Coke."

The two walked out of the house, holding their drinks as they approached the garden. Julia stood when she heard them approach and she wiped her brow with the back of her hand.

"I'm glad to see you guys are back," she said. "The weatherman on the radio says there could be a bad storm moving this way, maybe even a tornado or two."

They all instinctively looked to the west at the line of cumulous clouds. The clouds had grown taller since Eric last looked, and they were turning darker.

"Well, I'm going to get me a shower and then have another beer," Olaf announced. He turned and walked to the house, leaving Eric and Julia in the garden.

"Eric, if you could grab that bag of lettuce I won't have to come back." Julia smiled as she picked up a basket of carrots she had picked.

"Sure thing," Eric said. "Need a hand with anything else?"

Nope," Julie replied. "That'll do it."

Eric followed her to the house, his eyes fixed on her moving buttocks, perfectly outlined in her shorts as she walked. Her long, slender legs were tanned, almost brown, and her blond hair was bouncing on her shoulders as she walked.

He was so focused on Julia's backside that he stumbled on a rock, flying forward. The lettuce flew out of the bag as Eric skidded on the ground, scraping his chin.

Julia turned and rushed back, bending over him.

"Are you okay?" she asked.

"Yea, I'm all right," Eric said.

"Well I see you got a scrape on your chin so let's go in the house and I'll clean it up."

As they walked toward the house, they heard a rumble, far off in the distance. "Uff da," Julia said. "I don't like that sound coming from so far away. These storm warnings make me nervous."

They heard more thunder as they stepped into the house. Julia asked Eric to sit on a chair and she leaned over him to wash his bruised chin. She reached into a first-aid kit and retrieved a bottle of iodine.

"This will hurt a little," she said. She placed one hand on the side of Eric's face and with her other hand she gently brushed the iodine on his chin. Eric's body tightened and he felt a sharp sting his chin from the iodine. Julia smoothed a bandage across the cut and patted Eric's leg.

"You're good to go," she said, smiling.

"Thanks," Eric said as he stood and quickly walked out of the kitchen.

Eric went upstairs and took a shower, and as he

stepped out onto the bathroom floor there was a sudden, loud clap of thunder. An ear-shattering boom shook the house.

Suddenly the door to the bathroom flew open.

"Hurry up," Olaf said, grabbing Eric's arm. "Get your clothes on; we've got to get down to the basement. The storm is here!" Eric pulled on his pants and they rushed down to the basement door. Eric was pulling on his shirt as they made their way down the stairs.

Julia stood on the basement floor, pacing back and forth in front of the washing machine. "They say you should stand in the northwest corner of the basement," she said, herding Olaf and Eric toward that corner. "That's the safest place if a tornado comes and takes the house." Julia's face was dark and worried, just like Olaf.

They all stood nervously in the corner, waiting. The noise from the wind was growing louder each second, and soon it turned into a deafening roar. Eric could see Julia's mouth open wide shouting something, but he couldn't hear a word. The roar was growing even louder.

Eric thought he felt the house shaking harder as they stood in the corner looking up. The basement was lit by a single light bulb, dangling from a cord in the center of the room. The bulb began to sway as the house shook, and then suddenly it went dark.

They three drew closer in the darkness. The storm raged above them, a constant roaring noise, punctuated by shrieking winds. As the sounds of the storm grew even louder, they seemed to coalesce into a loud screaming howl.

Eric felt his body shudder; there was something about the sound of the storm that was terrifying and familiar.

They huddled closer as the house continued to shake. Eric raised his head in the darkness. He wondered what it might look like if the house were suddenly lifted up from the foundation.

Would the tornado suck us up too? Eric wondered. *Would it carry us high into the sky and then drop us to our deaths?*

Both Julia and Olaf's arms were now wrapped around him. They had moved into a tight huddle.

The ear-piercing, screaming wind sent more shudders moving down Eric's spine. And then he suddenly realized what was so familiar about the screaming wind. He'd hear the sounds of this storm before, the howling wind, the roar and the shrieking, screaming wind. It was the same sounds he heard that winter day on Ragged Butte when the blizzard forced him and his friends into the cave.

Now, as he cringed in their huddle in the basement, Eric marveled at his sudden realization: two deadly storms, one spawned in stifling summer heat and the other in frigid winter cold.

And they sounded exactly alike, Eric thought, *and now I'm underground again, seeking shelter.*

Eric tightened his hold on Julia and Olaf as the storm raged above. The deafening roar was growing as the wind battered the house. The screaming wind grew louder. They all moved closer in their huddle as though they were expecting a terrible finale.

The house was shaking so hard that dust began filtering down; the air became musty and suffocating. There was a sudden sharp ripping noise above, but it was quickly drowned out by the screaming wind.

Eric's ear's suddenly popped.

The abrupt silence that followed seemed a welcome escape from the terrifying sounds, but moments later Eric's ears popped again, and the howling sounds of the storm were back, the screaming wind pounding the house.

Eric's body began to shake. *How long can this house hold out?* He wondered.

They heard a crashing noise above them and the floor shook. It sounded like a terrible new phase of this storm was about to begin.

But then they heard a subtle change above them. It sounded like the screaming winds were dropping a bit. They stood very still, anxiously listening as the winds continued to diminish. The storm definitely was changing; they could all hear it.

The screaming sounds vanished, and now they heard only the gusting wind. And within a few minutes the wind gusts stopped, an eerie calm settling over the house.

They stood motionless, their bodies still tense, unsure if the storm was really gone. Julia was the first to speak. "I think it's gone," she said cautiously. "I think we're going to be okay."

As they stood in the dark, Julia drew closer until her face pressed tightly against Eric's cheek. She was pulling them into a three-person embrace. Olaf's stubble face pressed Eric's other cheek as they all hugged.

Then Julia began to cry very softly, a barely audible whimper that Olaf and Eric would not have heard if they had not been standing in the quiet darkness.

"It's okay," Olaf said in a soothing voice. "We're okay now. We're going to be all right." There was break in Olaf's voice as he spoke.

As they emerged from the basement, they saw the kitchen floor littered with broken glass, but the walls and ceiling were intact. The dish rack and several jars and containers were strewn across the floor. On the side of the kitchen, the door to the outside lay broken on the floor, apparently forced open by the winds.

Julia made her way through the debris and rushed out of the house to her garden. The corn was gone, the stalks completely ripped from the ground. The tomatoes were also gone, with just a few torn vines still on the ground. The rows of peas had disappeared.

Only the carrots and potatoes survived, safely anchored in the ground.

"It could have been much worse," Julia said as she raised her head and looked over the farm.

Olaf and Eric set out to examine the barn and their livestock. Fifteen minutes later they returned to the house, where Julia was sweeping the broken glass from the kitchen floor.

"Well, the barn seems to be okay, with just some minor damage" Olaf said. He sounded both pleased and surprised. "I thought the barn would be the first thing to go, but it held fast. And the livestock are spooked, but they're all right."

Olaf and Eric lifted the broken door from the floor and leaned it against the wall.

"I'm guessing the tornado passed over the farm without actually touching the ground." Olaf said. "I've heard that tornadoes sometimes do that."

Olaf brushed his hands on his pants and went to the refrigerator. He opened the door and took out three beers, handing one to Julia and one to Eric who looked very surprised. Then Olaf snapped the tab and opened his can.

"Go ahead, Eric, and drink it. I want all of us to participate in this toast," he said. Olaf raised his beer and took a big drink. Then Eric and Julia snapped open their cans and returned the toast.

"Just don't go home at the end of summer and tell your folks we were feeding you beer out here," Olaf told Eric. They all laughed loudly and then they made another toast to each other. It felt really good to laugh as they stood in Julia's shattered kitchen.

Olaf looked at the pile of broken glass in the middle of the floor and his face grew more serious.

"It could have been much worse if the tornado had dropped down to the ground," he said. "Damn tornados. If it ain't one thing it's another. There's always something brewing in the North Dakota weather, something that can destroy you."

Olaf raised his eyes from the broken glass and his face

softened as he looked at Julia.

"But we're lucky as hell," he said. "Our farm is still here and we're alive."

The plane appeared suddenly, swooping down over the farm before rising and circling wide above the valley then diving down again.

Olaf, Julia and Eric rushed out of the kitchen, leaving their breakfasts on the table, when they heard it pass overhead. They stood, shielding their eyes from the morning sun to watch the plane.

"It's Howard Olson," Olaf said. "He just got his license last week."

The small plane made another pass over the house then dipped to the ground, landing on the dirt road leading to the house.

The Piper Cub was white with a large blue stripe down its side. Its silver propeller continued spinning as the plane taxied up to the house. Then the engine died and the propeller stopped. The door under the wing flew open, and out stepped Howard Olson.

"Hey Olaf, howdy Julia, how do you like my new toy?" Howard asked as he stood grinning. Howard, who was short in height for a Scandinavian, could easily walk under the wing. His face had the weathered look of an older farmer and he wore coveralls and a crumpled hat, which he removed as he approached.

"Come into the house," Julia said. "We were having breakfast."

"Well, I didn't mean to interrupt your breakfast," he said. "But I could always use a cup of your coffee." Howard smiled warmly at Julia.

They went into the kitchen, and Julia pulled an extra chair to the table for Howard. Olaf and Eric finished eating their breakfast while Julia poured Howard a cup of coffee.

"I've always wanted one of these Piper Cubs," Howard said. "Last year's crop was pretty good, so I said, 'What the hell,' and I went out and bought one."

Olaf and Julia seemed to nod at one another. They had known Howard for a long time and knew he had a reputation of being impulsive. He did whatever he liked whenever he liked.

Of course this could be a bad trait for a farmer on the plains, and sometimes Howard's profit margins suffered. Like the spring he went fishing in Canada, seeded his crop two weeks late and missed the spring rains. Some of his wheat that year only yielded 10 to 15 bushels per acre, while his neighbors got 20 to 30 bushels.

Still, Howard owned so much land, rumored to be more than 4,000 acres, that when he had a good year on his farm he made so much money that it covered the bad years — and still left him with plenty of money to do whatever he wanted.

And so his lifestyle would continue, with Howard always making new plans for another fishing trip in Canada, or perhaps even Mexico. And it was likely his newest adventure would disrupt the normal farm schedule once again and make another dent in the next year's profit.

"What the hell do I care?" Howard said as he took a big drink of coffee. "This year I said I'm going to buy me a plane, so I did it."

He smiled again. "I went down to Fargo last winter and bought my Piper Cub from another farmer. The farmer flew it up from Fargo three days ago, landing in the pasture in front of our house. I took him to the train station the next morning so he could catch the Great Northern back to Fargo."

"What about your license?" Julia asked.

"I took flying lessons last winter up at Sloan Field in Williston, I passed the test a month ago, and Bismarck mailed me my license. So now I'm all set to fly off into the wild blue yonder, maybe even clear up into Canada to go fishing."

"Are you going to use it for anything else?" Olaf asked.

"Hell, I don't know," Howard said. "You know, my place is pretty good size. The plane might come in handy to fly around and keep tabs on my sheep; see where they're grazing."

"But right now I'm just trying to keep the damn thing up in the air."

They all laughed and Julia got the coffee pot and filled their cups again.

"So anyhow, I thought I'd stop by here and give my neighbors a ride," Howard said, moving his head around the table. "I think we can all fit."

"Not me," Julia responded. "I don't like to fly." Julia spoke like a seasoned traveler, but everyone knew she had been on an airplane only once, a Frontier Airline "puddle jumper" that flew from Williston to Denver, stopping at a half dozen towns along the way. By the time Julia arrived in Denver to visit her sister, she was already making plans for her return trip home — by bus.

Howard nodded politely at Julia, who was still smiling but slowly shaking her head no. Howard turned to Olaf and Eric. "Okay, let's go," he said. "This will be a flight for men only."

They got into the cockpit, Eric seated between Howard and Olaf. The doors slammed shut and Howard started the engine.

"Fasten your seat belts," Howard said. "We're going up." He pointed skyward with his right thumb.

The engine revved up as the plane turned and faced down the road. Howard increased the engine speed until suddenly the plane began moving down the road, steadily gaining speed until it lifted up. They could see the county road dropping away below them, and then Howard turned the plane to make a pass over the farm.

Julia stood waving in front of the house, a tiny figure far below.

The plane was still gaining altitude as it passed over the Halvorson's north pasture.

"Yeeeeeehaaaaaa!" Howard shouted, a big smile on his face as he turned to look at Olaf and Eric. "Ain't this fun?"

Howard banked the plane to the left and the plane leveled off as they headed due west. They were flying directly over Howard's land. The prairie stretched below in a broad expanse of green and brown. Several cultivated and seeded fields soon appeared, a small patchwork bordered by more prairie.

Howard dropped the plane lower. "That's my biggest field," he shouted, pointing to a 160-acre square of green. "It's all durum, so I'm hoping to get a good price."

As the plane continued west, it passed over Howard's massive pasture land. Howard's sheep roamed free on the grassland. "My sheep produced lots of lambs down there this spring, but I lost a few newborns to those damn eagles." he said, shaking his head in disgust.

"You sure it was eagles?" Olaf asked.

"I'm damn sure it was eagles," Howard said. "I see them circling above the pasture all the time."

"Well, it could be coyotes," Olaf said. "Or maybe even a cougar. Some ranchers have recently spotted cougars coming up the Badlands."

"Nope, it's eagles." Howard shouted the words so he could be heard above the noise of the plane's engine. "One of my ewes had a stillborn so I spiked it with poison and laid it on top of a hill. Sure enough, a couple days later I checked it and there was a dead eagle nearby that had been eating it. It was a big male, with a seven-foot wing span. Hell, he could have picked up a ewe and flown away."

"Well, eagles are scavengers so if they see a dead animal they'll stop to feed on it," Olaf said. "But it doesn't mean the eagle has been killing your lambs. And now you've made a female eagle a widow."

Howard laughed until he saw Olaf didn't intend it to be a joke.

"Did you know that eagles mate for life?" Olaf continued. "Both the male and female watch over their eaglets, and they bring them food. I read that in a book."

Howard's face was turning dark and somber. Olaf sensed he had said enough and turned to look out the window.

Howard, however, always felt the need to have the last word. He cleared his voice to get Olaf's full attention before speaking. "Well, as the sheep ranchers say, 'the only good eagle is a dead eagle.' "

"Whatever," Olaf mumbled, almost under his breath.

The plane crossed over the breaks leading down to the Yellowstone River and then passed over the Fairview Bridge.

As they passed over the span, Eric remembered his frightening attempt to climb the bridge tower and the frenzied run through the railroad tunnel, chased by the Goose. He smiled just a little as he looked down, trying to see where Charbonneau Creek flew into the Yellowstone.

It seemed like that day was a very long time ago, and now Eric sat confidently in a Piper Cub, high above it all.

Howard turned the plane in a wide circle, and soon they were flying east again. The Yellowstone River breaks passed underneath and the rolling grassland appeared below once again.

"Son of a bitch!" Howard shouted the words and quickly turned his head to look out the side window. "Did you see that?"

"What is it?" Olaf asked.

"I think I just saw another damn eagle," Howard said.

Olaf and Eric leaned forward to look while Howard banked the plane, turning into a wide circle. Howard reached his left arm behind the seat and pulled out a shotgun, banging the barrel against the window.

"I'm going to get that son of a bitch!" Howard's face was filled with hate.

Olaf reached across the seat to tap Howard on his shoulder "I don't think that's a good idea." Olaf's shouted. "It's illegal and I don't think it's safe to be shooting a 16 gauge up here."

Howard's face was unchanged and determined. "Hang on," he shouted as the plane began to descend.

It was then that Eric spotted the eagle flying alongside the plane, its giant wings moving gracefully in a forward motion. Eric's body grew tense as Howard maneuvered the plane closer.

Turn back, dive down, get away from the plane, Eric thought.

There was a sudden rush of air into the cockpit as Howard lowered his side window and thrust the shotgun barrel through the opening. Eric felt the urge to grab the shotgun and pull it away from Howard. *But what if Howard resisted? What if he lost control of the plane?*

Time seemed to stand still as Olaf and Eric watched Howard train his shotgun on the eagle.

The sudden shotgun blast shook the plane, and a cloud of feathers burst from the eagle.

"Yeeeehaaaaaaaa!" Howard shouted as he rolled up the plane window. "I got that son of as bitch!"

The hate was gone from Howard's face, replaced by morbid joy. He banked the plane so they could see the eagle's body plunging to earth in a gruesome, rolling motion, its giant wings flapping in all directions.

Eric turned and stared silently at Olaf for a moment. Olaf slowly shook his head in silence and then looked out the window again at the falling eagle. The stench of gunpowder filled the cockpit.

"I can't believe I shot that eagle," Howard boasted. "We were just talking about those goddamn eagles and there it was. How lucky is that? Yeeeehaaaaa!"

Howard seemed to be deep in his happy thoughts as he leveled off the Piper Cub for their flight back.

"I just discovered one more thing I can do with my plane," he said.

Olaf and Eric were silent during the flight back to the farm. Howard seemed oblivious to the expressions on their faces as he did all the talking.

"Well, there's one less eagle to flying around here to menace my lambs," he said. They circled once over the Halvorson farm, and Howard lowered the plane to land on the roadway. The plane bounced once as it touched the road and then settled down again and taxied up to the farmhouse.

Julia came out of the house. The warm smile on her face began to fade when she saw the expressions on Olaf's and Eric's faces.

"I shot a damn eagle, they've been taking my lambs," Howard said as he stepped out of his plane.

"How did you do that?" Julia asked.

"I carry a 16 gauge in my plane," Howard said, motioning toward the Piper Cub. "I blasted that son of a bitch right out of midflight!"

Julia stood almost transfixed by what she was hearing.

"My God, Howard, isn't that dangerous? Julia asked. "Isn't that illegal?"

"Shit no, it ain't illegal if no one sees you do it," Howard said.

Olaf and Eric climbed out of the plane and walked past Howard toward the house.

"Okay, Olaf, I'll be seeing you," Howard said, raising his hand in a sign he was leaving.

Olaf turned toward Howard and raised his arm. "Okay, see you," he said with a slight wave.

The eagle's nest was perched on a rocky outcropping on the side of a steep butte. The day was sunny and bright and the eaglets were beginning to stir in the nest. The mother eagle suddenly stretched her wings and slowly lifted up from her nest, the downdraft ruffling her eaglets' tiny feathers. As the mother eagle rose higher she glanced back for one more look at her eaglets, their tiny heads barely visible above the sides of the nest. The mother eagle gained altitude as she flew south to her favorite hunting ground, the prairie dog colony. As she arrived above the colony she dropped lower and began a slow circling motion, searching for a target. But suddenly she was interrupted by a strange noise. Turning, she saw a shiny white object with a spinning motion in front. Then there was a bright yellow flash ...

Eric awakened with a jolt, sitting up in his bed, breathing heavily. He glanced through his room at the window and realized it was a dream. He got out of bed and walked to the window and leaned out to breathe the night air. A thin slice of the moon had risen above the hills. The air was warm and very still.

Normally he would have savored this moment when the prairie stood silent, at peace with itself. But Eric knew there was no peace on the prairie this evening. As he looked out at the night sky, he felt a nagging awareness of doom. Something terrible would soon happen in this beautiful and tranquil place.

As Eric looked up at the moon and stars, he could only imagine one scene. Somewhere out there on the prairie was a nest perched on a rocky outcropping. The nest was filled with eaglets. The eaglets were hungry and they were calling for their mother.

"Want some bacon and eggs?" Julia asked as Eric came into the kitchen.

"Yes, please," he replied, "it sounds good."

Olaf entered the room and sat at the table.

"I've got to run to town today to order some parts for the tractor and combine," he said. "I don't know how long I'll be gone, so I was thinking you could probably saddle up Cody and ride down to the south pasture and check the fence line, just like we did up north."

Eric shook his head yes, trying not to look too excited over the day's work assignment.

"You'll probably be gone for most of the day, so Julia will make you some lunch to take along."

Eric devoured his breakfast, excused himself and headed to the barn.

Cody whinnied loudly when she saw him approach the corral. The two had developed a friendly bond that summer, with Eric often riding Cody up in the hills at night before sunset.

Eric went into the barn and got the saddle and bridle. Cody stood perfectly still as he saddled her up. She seemed to sense they were going for a long ride and she was anxious to get going.

The trail stretched south from the farm for a half mile and then began to climb up a bank of low hills where the south pasture was. There was no creek to follow on this trail from the farm, only a worn pathway through the grass.

Later that morning they came upon a small pond, so

Eric stopped, dismounted and led Cody to the water. The day was growing very hot. It seemed as though this heat wave would never end.

After the pause to drink they continued on to the south pasture. Eric dismounted, opened the wire gate and led Cody through. As soon as he climbed up in the saddle, Cody moved over to the fence line and began following it. She knew exactly what they were going to do that day.

As they began sauntering down along the line of fence, Eric leaned forward and patted Cody on the side, and he relaxed the reins so she could walk at her own pace.

They soon came to some loose wire, so Eric dismounted and unfastened the tool bag from the saddle. Eric stretched the wire tightly and refastened it. Standing back, he briefly admired the tightened wire on the fence before mounting Cody. Then they continued to follow the fence line.

"You're a good horse," Eric said rubbing the side of her neck.

Cody turned and whinnied loudly, and Eric laughed. Cody was the most talkative horse he had ever known.

By noontime, Eric estimated they had covered approximately half of the fence surrounding the giant pasture. The day was growing hotter, and he began to search for water and shade. Soon he spotted a manmade embankment on the side up a hill with the tops of cottonwoods rising above the embankment. The dark green cottonwoods stood out on the dry prairie, which was beginning to turn brown. They rode up over the embankment to the dam's reservoir, which was nearly empty. Only a small pool of water remained in the middle, surrounded by hard, cracked earth.

Approaching the pond, Eric dismounted, leading Cody to the water. She bent and took a long drink, then raised her head to look at a solitary frog swimming in the water.

Eric unfastened his water bag and lunch sack and left Cody at the pool to drink. He walked to the edge of the cracked earth where the cottonwoods stood. Finding a flat area, he smoothed the grass with his boots.

"Doesn't hurt to be careful," he said out loud to himself. "You never know when a rattler might be lingering in the grass."

He sat down on the grass, thinking about what he had just done.

Yeah, I just had a conversation with myself, he thought. *I've been doing a lot of that this summer. But who else is there to talk to out here, other than Cody?*

"And she's a horse," he said out loud, laughing at himself.

Eric reached in his saddlebag and pulled out a roast beef sandwich. He was pleased to see how big the sandwich was as he took his first bite. He ate in silence, glancing down at Cody, who was still down at the pond sipping the water and stopping occasionally to stare at the frog. Cody was not only the most talkative horse in the world, she was also the most curious.

Eric finished the sandwich and reached back in the lunch bag, pulling out an apple and small bag of pretzels.

He began munching on the apple and called for Cody. "Come on girl, "he said. "There's some nice grass for you to eat over here."

Cody walked carefully across the baked floor of the reservoir to the tall grass and began grazing. Then she suddenly froze, raised her head and sniffed the air. She caught the smell of the apple and turned to approach Eric.

"No, you can't have any," he teased. "It's all mine." Eric hunched his body over the apple so Cody couldn't see it; Cody nudged his shoulder with her nose.

Eric stood laughing and unfolded his hand. "Okay, girl, you can have what's left."

Cody spread her lips wide and carefully bit into the apple. As Eric pulled his hand away to wipe the horse slobber on his pants, pieces of apple fell onto the grass. Cody finished chewing her mouthful, then began carefully picking up each loose piece of apple from the grass. Then she sauntered back to the tall grass and continued grazing.

Eric lay back in the shade of the cottonwoods and closed his eyes for a moment. The heat of the day and his full stomach were making him sleepy.

I better not take a nap, he thought. *Cody might wander off.*

He took a long drink from his water bag. Then he got up and mounted Cody. They rode down the hill to the fence line and began slowly following it once again.

The air felt much hotter out in the open sun, away

from the shade of the cottonwoods. Eric tilted his hat against the sun and loosened the reins again so Cody could proceed at her own pace.

They crossed the top of a large hill and followed the fence down into a broad valley. The Halvorsons had not yet moved any of their cattle to this pasture for summer grazing, so the grass was high, especially as Eric and Cody neared the bottom of the valley.

Suddenly, Eric noticed the grass moving in a thrashing motion up ahead. As they drew closer the grass suddenly stood still.

"They've heard us or they've smelled us," Eric whispered to Cody. "They know we're here."

Cody whinnied back, much louder than Eric wanted.

"Shhh," he whispered. "Let's see if we can get a little closer."

They slowly moved forward, the only sound coming from Cody's hoofs moving through the grass.

Suddenly three large coyotes darted out of the tall grass and began running up the hillside, their long tails flopping behind them. In a few moments they reached the top and disappeared over the ridge.

Eric dismounted and led Cody forward. The grass was waist high and difficult to move through. Suddenly Eric stepped out of the tall grass into a circle where the grass was flattened to the ground. A tiny lamb lay dead in the middle, surrounded by streaks of blood mixed with wool and matted into the grass. At the edge of the flattened grass Eric spotted one small leg, obviously torn from the lamb.

Eric turned and suddenly threw up into the tall grass; then he dropped to his knees and threw up again. He slowly stood and turned, trying not to look directly at the mutilated carcass. Cody stood above the lamb, gently sniffing its lifeless body.

Eric called to Cody and she walked over to him. He unfastened the water bag from the side and rinsed the acrid taste from his mouth. Then he took a long drink, all the while ignoring the dead lamb.

He stepped back and surveyed the area once more, glancing briefly at the carcass. Then he mounted Cody and they rode out of the tall grass to the fence and began following the line once again.

As they followed the fence, Eric looked to the south where the hills flattened out onto a broad plain. Elling Gullickson's farm was a half mile in that direction; the fence was the boundary between the Halvorson and Gullickson farms.

The Gullicksons had hundreds of sheep; their farm was most likely where the lamb came from. Eric thought of how small the mutilated lamb appeared; it was a tiny creature that could quickly disappear in the tall prairie grass. As Eric looked down at the fence he realized the little lamb probably wandered away from its mother and crossed under the lowest wire on the fence.

For such a small, fragile animal, an innocent stroll away from its mother could quickly become fatal. The prairie appeared peaceful and safe, but Eric knew it could also be a very dangerous place, especially for little creatures.

One moment the little lamb was probably frolicking in the grass. Then, in an instant, the coyotes pounced on it and began tearing it to pieces.

As Eric and Cody began climbing the hill on the other side of the valley, still following the fence, Eric knew the coyotes were watching him from the far ridge, eagerly waiting to return to their gruesome feast.

When they reached the top of the hill, Eric pulled Cody to a stop and they turned to look down into the valley. He could barely distinguish the tiny lamb's white carcass in the grass.

Eric shook his head at what he had just seen. The mutilated lamb was a gruesome sight, made worse by knowing the repercussions that would follow if the rancher discovered it. All predators in the area would have marks on their backs, whether they had been attacking the Gullickson's sheep or not.

Howard Olson's farm bordered the Gullickson farm on the west. The coyotes were likely the same predators that took Howard's lamb. And a mother eagle paid the price.

Eric felt the anger grow within him as he remembered Howard blasting the eagle from his plane.

Howard the eagle murderer, Eric thought. *Howard the eaglet murderer.*

He spat on the ground in disgust.

Still, Eric knew that Howard was no worse than others. For the farmers and ranchers, survival was all that mattered, even if you took an innocent creature's life.

This was their belief, a faith passed down from the first homesteaders who knew how to survive on this wild, untamed land. If there was anything that threatened their livestock, anything that *might* threaten their livestock, they killed it. This was the only sure way to survive, and this creed would continue to be passed down from generation to generation by the most stubborn people on earth.

Eric spat on the ground again, prompting Cody to turn her head and whinny at him.

Eric chuckled at his horse and shrugged his shoulders. "Okay, girl, let's go home." They turned for the long ride back to the Halvorson farm. As he rode, Eric looked out over the sun-baked prairie. He imagined he could almost see the grass turning browner in the furnace-like heat.

Eric wondered what thoughts might have crept into the homesteaders' minds on a blazing hot day like this. As the homesteader struggled behind a team of oxen, maneuvering a single plow across the dusty prairie, did he reminisce about life back in Norway? Maybe he remembered casting a fishing line in a cool mountain lake?

While many Norwegian Americans held onto their parents' stories of life in the "old country," others such as Howard did not. Those who discarded the tales of life in the Norway became shaped entirely by the prairie and the new culture that was born on the prairie. It was a culture based on survival; a society that would quickly destroy anything that threatened it.

As he rode down the trail, deep in his thoughts, there was one question that kept nagging him.

Was this what the prairie did to the people who lived here? Eric wondered.

He looked out over the rolling hills. Heat waves were moving across the hilltops. The air was hot to breathe and his shirt was wet with sweat. He reached down for his water bag and took a long drink. Then he pulled Cody to a stop and looked closer at the land. He realized there was no shade, not a single tree in sight. The prairie suddenly looked unfriendly, even threatening.

Eric leaned forward and patted Cody on the side of her head, a move intended to comfort himself as much as his horse. Then they continued down the trail.

And for the first time in his life, Eric questioned whether he would stay in this land forever.

Chapter 7

40 years later

A sharp cracking noise split the air, followed by an ear-shattering boom. The room shook as though something heavy had dropped on the floor, rattling the windows. Eric's eye's opened, trying to focus on the strange noise and surroundings.

A dull roar was growing louder outside his window. Then another long cracking noise sliced through the room, followed by thunder. The windows were still rattling, and it sounded as though the room were being shaken loose.

Eric stared up at the ceiling for a moment before remembering where he was. He was in his sister Clarice's house in Alexander. The room had unfamiliar blue walls with dark wooden frames around the windows.

It was early morning, his last day in Alexander. As he swung out of bed, another burst of thunder shook the building. He looked out the bedroom window as lightning laced above the hills to the west. His eyes caught some movement in a grove of cottonwoods below the house. Four antelope stepped out from the trees, sniffed the air and then trotted up toward the house. The antelope stopped below the window, and suddenly they all leaped forward, sprinting up the nearby hill with incredible speed.

Eric stood watching their strange leaping, bouncing

motion. In a few moments they reached the top of the hill and disappeared over the ridge. It seemed like a fitting icon to see on his last day in North Dakota. It would be hard to imagine this land without the antelope, their lean, muscular bodies running across the prairie. They were survivors, even at the turn of the 20th century when the buffalo were slaughtered to near extinction. Now, as Eric looked out his window, he was sure the antelope would be there forever.

The hillside was empty now, with only the wind pushing the grass in waves across the slope while dark clouds were forming above.

The day was beginning on a stormy note. The skies were turning darker as the wind increased and another sharp crack of thunder sliced through the air. Then the thunder sounded, shaking the house again. It was a typical Dakota storm, appearing suddenly, growing quickly and spreading a dark shadow over the prairie. At any moment it would begin pouring rain or maybe hail. Another sharp cracking noise pierced the air, and thunder shook the house again, rattling the windows.

Large raindrops began pelting the window with sharp pinging sounds, and then sheets of rain suddenly poured down. Eric marveled at the intensity of the storm. He had watched prairie thunderstorms like this a hundred times before, but it was so long ago that he almost forgot how quickly the storms formed and how powerful they became.

Torrential rain was pouring down the window and the cottonwoods were bent by the howling wind. The storm was giving the prairie a real pounding outside his window. Still, Eric knew this thunderstorm would soon pass and the winds would calm. The cottonwoods would sway back to their upright positions, and the prairie would have a fresh new scent that was pleasing to breath. In a very short while, the resilient prairie would look like nothing had happened.

The prairie, like the people that inhabited it, endured whatever Mother Nature sent its way. The people who could not accept this life would simply leave.

Eric was one of those who left. After graduating from the university he headed west to a newspaper job in Washington. Eventually he moved south to California, where he married and raised a family.

And now, 40 years after leaving, Eric returned to attend the Alexander High School Reunion. Because of the small size of the school, all graduates from any year were invited. At the beginning of the two-day reunion, hundreds of alumni showed up at the city park bordering Main Street. Eric was waiting in line to register when a man wearing jeans, a western shirt and cowboy hat approached.

"I'll be damned," the man said. His face had the dark, weathered look of a rancher or farmer. "Are you still out there in la-la land?" he asked.

Eric grinned back, and shook his head yes, trying not to look confused. He had no idea who this man was.

"You're a spitting image of your old man," the cowboy continued. He paused a moment, removing his hat to mop his forehead with the palm of his hand. His hair was blonde, giving him a much younger look without the hat.

"Lee Anderson?" Eric asked.

"That's right," he said. "It's been a long time, hasn't it? Graduation night, I think."

Eric's mind was racing now, trying to remember as much as he could about his former classmate.

"Uh, yeah," he said. "I guess it was graduation night."

Lee was one of the few in Eric's graduating class who stayed in North Dakota. He owned a 4,000-acre ranch southwest of town, which straddled Charbonneau Creek. Lee was the only son in his family, and therefore, the ranch was destined to be his. Neither of his two sisters had ever thought, or dared to imagine, that the land would go to anyone else. Consequently, Lee's future was decided long before graduation, almost as though he had no choice on the matter. The unwritten rule of the land meant the ranch would become Lee's ranch; he would hold it until he grew old and then he would give it to his son.

Lee seemed to pause, as if he were reading Eric's thoughts. "You remember our graduation, don't you?" he asked, a grin spreading across his face.

"I sure do," Eric said.

Eric recalled that night in 1962 when the graduates converged on the home of classmate Jim Gunderson following their commencement ceremony. The cars had been moved out of the Gunderson's garage, and classmates decorated the interior with crepe paper and Japanese lanterns. In the corner, a ragged-looking tiki bar stood with two stools in front. Behind the bar was a keg of beer.

A record player sat on a table, playing rock 'n' roll music. The garage was crammed with graduates and their girlfriends, boyfriends and friends from neighboring towns.

The party was growing louder as the teenagers danced to the music. Others stood at the tiki bar, waiting to fill their paper cups with beer. The graduation party was intended to be an all-night affair, and no one planned to go home until the sun came up.

As the party went on, the air in the garage became warm and smoky. About 4 a.m. Eric went outside to get some air. Eric was strolling across the grass in the darkness when he heard noises nearby. He stopped to listen. Did someone fall and get hurt? Or maybe someone was lying on the grass, sick after drinking too much?

"Hey, anyone there?" he said. There was no answer.

He was slowly moving forward, trying to find the noise, when he stepped on something.

"Ouch! Son of a bitch! Get off my hand!"

Eric raised his foot and stepped backward. He pulled his cigarette lighter from his pocket and when he lit it the light shined on Lee and his girlfriend Jenny who were lying on the grass.

Now, decades later, Eric's face blushed as he and Lee stood grinning at each other in Alexander Park.

"Well, I'll be seeing you later," Lee said. "Maybe we can get together and have a beer and reminisce some of the good old days."

"Yeah, that would be good," Eric said.

As Eric wandered through the park he met several people from his high school days, some of whom he had not seen since their graduation. Most of Eric's classmates, like himself, went off to college and never returned.

Many of those who left had simply grown tired of the long, cold winters. Others dreamed of a new and exciting life in the city, far from the sparsely populated prairie.

Some of Eric's classmates who later graduated from college might have stayed in North Dakota had they found jobs. But North Dakota's mostly rural environment offered limited professional opportunities.

Now, Eric felt almost like a stranger here in his hometown. And yet, despite the many years that had passed since he called this place home, he also felt a vague familiarity with the town that seemed to grow within him as he strolled the dusty streets, searching for familiar homes and faces.

He walked down the alley leading from Main Street to where his family's house once stood. The house was gone, and there was only an empty lot covered by weeds and thinning grass with a single cottonwood off to one side. Bordering the lot where the house once stood was the half-acre grassy area that Eric used as a summer pasture for Moonlight.

The half-acre was still empty, and Eric walked to the middle. He didn't want to think about that terrible day, but as he stood in the middle of the grassy area, everything looked too familiar to forget what happened there. Eric stared at the far corner where Moonlight frantically ran into the barbed wire fence, chased by the mongrel dog. Eric would never forget the gruesome site of Moonlight cartwheeling through the air, wrapped in the wire, and crashing into the ground.

Eric's much-loved horse lay there in tremendous pain, unable to move. Moonlight would have watched as two men arrived and carried the unconscious Eric away on a stretcher. Eric's father approached Moonlight and began cutting the wire and slowly unwrapping it from her body. He might have stroked the crescent on Moonlight's head as he worked to free her.

Finally, the last of the wire was removed and he urged Moonlight to stand. She slowly rose to her feet, shook her head and whinnied softly. Her dark eyes looked dazed as he examined her body. He shook his head when he saw her right front leg hanging loose from her body. The leg was broken, and there was nothing he could do to save her.

Moments later Moonlight's life ended. Now, as Eric stood on the site, he could imagine his father leveling the end of his 16-gauge directly at Moonlight's head. The loud shotgun blast would be followed by Moonlight's body collapsing with a thud to the ground. His father would have kneeled over the collapsed horse to make sure she was dead.

As he recalled the horrific events of that day, Eric could only shake his head in disgust at what had happened. He turned and spit on the ground and began walking out of the pasture without looking back.

He picked up his pace as he continued walking down the street, anxious to see something different. But then he stopped and turned to look back at the former pasture one last time. The wind was picking up, moving the grass in waves across the half-acre.

Eric imagined his father standing over his dead horse. As his father turned to walk away, he probably wiped his eyes. "I'll never forget the look on your dad's face after he did it," Eric's mother had said. A guilty feeling swept over Eric as he pictured what likely happened.

On that terrible day, Eric's father found the strength to move beyond his own emotions and committed an atrocious act to end Moonlight's suffering. Eric responded to his father's selfless action with angry screams and a look of hatred.

Eric spit on the ground again and turned. He couldn't shake his guilt, so he began walking down the street again. It felt good to be moving away from grassy pasture. Slowly, his shame seemed to fade as he paid closer attention to the houses on the street. He noticed there were many empty lots scattered around town where homes once stood.

Alexander had fallen on rough times when the rural economy collapsed along with the prices for cattle and wheat. Many homes in town were simply abandoned as families left. Once a house stood empty for several years, it began to deteriorate in the harsh climate. Eventually the Town Council would order the dilapidated home demolished. It was better to see nothing on a quarter-acre lot than a weathered, crumbling home, a constant reminder of one more family that lost its struggle to live here.

Survival was always a constant struggle on the Northern Plains, and this extended to the small towns such as Alexander that dotted the landscape.

"People are getting old and dying, and the town is dying with them," Eric's sister said.

At first it seemed strange to Eric how easily his sister and the other locals seemed to accept the possibility that Alexander might soon become one more ghost town on the North Dakota prairie. But then, he reasoned, to live on the prairie is to accept what that land offered, or what the land didn't offer. It was useless to imagine anything else could happen.

Still, the townspeople's easy acceptance of their future, no matter what it would bring, seemed strange and fatalistic to Eric. As he strolled through the town, he sensed that he no longer belonged here. He was almost a stranger in this place. He felt a nagging, almost tense feeling in his stomach and even questioned why he had come to this reunion.

He walked past the school and followed the road up the hill toward the cemetery. As he followed the road out of town it dropped down into a low valley, with the Gunderson farm off to the left. Eric knew Jim's younger sister, Amie, lived there with her husband.

Eric continued walking past the farm and soon came to the cemetery, which sat on top a low hill below Tub Butte. A single gravel road entered the cemetery and wound its way through the gravesites. As Eric walked into the cemetery he could see Ragged Butte rising above the low hills to the northwest.

His parents' tombstones stood side by side near the

middle of the cemetery. The gravesites seemed like a strange resting place for Justin and Inga Anderson. Something just didn't look right to Eric as he looked at their names chiseled into the heavy, unmoving stone. He thought his parents might not appreciate this stationary plot on the hillside. After all, they were prairie nomads for so many years, and although they often complained about having to move from one small town to the next, Eric always suspected they somewhat enjoyed it.

In fact, Eric's parents resumed their nomadic ways once Eric and his sisters had all grown up and left home. Their parents first moved to Flathead Lake in Montana where they bought a cherry farm. However, they soon grew tired of chasing deer and an occasional bear out of their orchard, so they sold the place. Then they moved back to North Dakota where Justin managed an elevator in Epping. When the dust in the elevator began to bother Justin, they moved again to Williston where they bought a health food store.

Eric's parents were not averse to new scenery, but now they would lie underground forever in this one spot. Eric shook his head at his thoughts. He wondered if perhaps it would have been better to cremate them and scatter their ashes in the prairie wind.

Who knows where their ashes might end up?

How appropriate would that be? Eric asked himself as a smile spread across his face.

He continued walking down the cemetery road until he came to Jim Gunderson's tombstone. Jim's tombstone looked like most of them, a thick slice of granite with a curved top. Jim's name was chiseled into the center of the stone with the dates of his birth and death below. There was no mention that Jim died in a car accident late one winter night near Watford City. He was only 25 years old.

Eric realized that of all the people buried in this cemetery, Jim was laid to rest the closest to his home. When Eric looked to the west from the cemetery he could see the tops of the cottonwood trees at the Gunderson farm. The cemetery sat squarely in the middle of the area where Eric and Jim had so often ridden Moonlight and Dandy.

Eric looked toward Ragged Butte. On a warm day like this, he and Jim would have ridden their horses to the top of the butte and then down to Jackson Lake for a swim. He had so many pleasant memories from this land, but now the land looked strange to him. He had forgotten the scope of the prairie, with the vast plains stretching to the horizon. Now when Eric looked at the land, it appeared empty, and the only movement was the breeze moving the grass in waves across the hilltops.

Eric continued walking on the road in the cemetery until he came to John Hanson's grave. John's tombstone was traditional with his name chiseled in the middle and the dates below. Like most of the tombstones, it did not reveal details of why John died at age 54.

John was the one those few who stayed in North Dakota. He earned a degree in agricultural engineering from the university, inherited his father's farm and also started a successful farm machinery business. He married and raised a family, building a large house down the road from his parents' farm. And then one day came word from his doctor that John had cancer, with only a few months to live. When Eric heard the news he telephoned John.

"I never abused my body a lot," John said. "Oh sure, I used to get drunk now and then, but not very often. I never smoked, except when others had cigarettes. And I worked out nearly every day in my weight room. And then it still got me ..."

It was an anguishing conversation between friends. They both struggled to maintain a normal voice as they talked. There was such finality to their conversation, and when they hung up it was the last time they ever talked.

Eric turned and continued walking down the cemetery road. He had one more gravesite to visit.

Ray Sorenson's tombstone was one of the strangest in the cemetery. It was made of rough stone, without the typical tombstone shape. From a distance it looked like a large rock had been dropped on the grass. As Eric approached the stone he saw Ray's name chiseled neatly at the bottom, along with his date of birth and death. In the center of the rough stone was a message: *I did it all and it was fun.*

A smile spread across Eric's face as he nodded at the rock. His eyes were becoming moist.

Ray the explorer went where many of his friends dared not go. He had no fear of the unknown and he had no fear of being different, even in death. Still, there was also something missing from Ray's tombstone; as with Jim and John's markers, Ray's tombstone did not reveal the details of his life and death.

Ray had graduated in international relations from the

university and had a successful career with the U.S. State Department. He died suddenly one morning of a heart attack as he walked to the corner market in his Georgetown neighborhood to buy a quart of milk. Ray's family held the funeral service in Washington, D.C.; then his body was flown 1,400 miles west to be buried here in the Alexander Cemetery per Ray's wishes.

As Eric stood at his gravesite, glancing up at Ragged Butte, he knew why Ray chose this spot.

Eric turned and began following the winding road out of the cemetery. When he reached the cemetery gate he stopped. The late afternoon sun was lower, casting a softer color on the prairie. The sandstone boulders on top Ragged Butte reflected an orange shine. Even the tombstones in the cemetery mirrored the soft afternoon sun, radiating certain warmth.

Eric knew he would remember this moment forever, standing at the cemetery gate. His parents and his friends were all buried here, and now only he was still alive.

The afternoon breeze was fading and the grass stood almost still. Eric could feel the sadness growing in him as he looked out over the prairie, the low, rolling hills stretching to the horizon. He scanned the hillsides but could not see a single person anywhere. It was such a lonely, yet beautiful sight.

"This was my Dakota." He said the words out loud in a firm voice as if to convince himself that he once lived there. He had once been part of this land, but now he felt detached from it.

Now he was a stranger there, and he could only dream of what once was.

CPSIA information can be obtained at www.ICGtesting.com
261234BV00006B/1/P